GILBERT SORRENTINO

Odd Number

NORTH POINT PRESS   SAN FRANCISCO

1985

Thus we have characters who are to be considered identical because they look alike. This relation is accented by mental processes leaping from one of these characters to another—by what we should call telepathy—, so that the one possesses knowledge, feelings and experience in common with the other. Or it is marked by the fact that the subject identifies himself with someone else, so that he is in doubt as to which his self is, or substitutes the extraneous self for his own. In other words, there is a doubling, dividing and interchanging of the self. And finally there is the constant recurrence of the same thing—the repetition of the same features or character-traits or vicissitudes, of the same crimes, or even the same names through several consecutive generations.

SIGMUND FREUD (The "Uncanny")

Odd Number

W as it still twilight, or had it already grown dark?

If you'll again permit me to get my notes in order, I'll   according to my data, what there is of it, it was not yet   quite dark, yet it was just past what is usually called twilight   certainly it was not yet dark enough not to be able to see, since it is clear that the three of them were seen in the street, beneath a plane tree   it was a soft evening late spring

The seating arrangement in the car?

Mr. Lewis was driving although the car was owned by Mr. Henry   owned   more or less   it was Mr. Henry's car   he owned the car, but not exactly outright, as these reports make clear   Mr. Lewis was driving, Mrs. Henry was seated next to him, and Mr. Henry was in the back seat   no one else was in the car

Earlier you mentioned, in passing, that there had been a lot of drinking. What sort of drinking?

I did? I don't remember saying that   was there a memo on that?   they had been drinking all afternoon but I have no evidence that they were drunk   perhaps a little high would be the word, the expression   after all, Mr. Lewis was driving, quite competently all right, all right!   Mr. Lewis had   thrown up   earlier in the day and Mrs. Henry had modeled a new   bathing suit   for her husband and Mr. Lewis   somebody took some   her husband had taken some photographs of her   I have two of them here, supposedly not a very good likeness but would you like to see them?   whatever informa- tion I have is yours

What was Sheila wearing?

Mrs. Henry was wearing a sleeveless shift of off-white raw silk, the hemline coming to just above the knees, a black-and-white-fig- ured rayon scarf knotted loosely about her neck, sheer nylon stockings of the shade called   just a moment   the shade called Smoke and black sling high-heeled shoes   I have an addendum on her underclothing but surely   good   yes, that would do it, standard standard feminine underclothing, fine   you can use your imagination   I don't mean you you

There have been persistent rumors that Lou Henry owed something to Guy Lewis and that this debt was the reason that Guy was tolerated as a more or less permanent guest in Lou's home. What, if anything, did Lou owe Guy?

It wasn't exactly a debt, as you put it, but more like   gratitude   it's well documented that Mr. Lewis did a series of linoleum cuts for Mr. Henry's first book, which was either   *Sheila Sleeping* or *The Orange*   no   or *Lobster Lays*   and that, further, he had arranged for its publication with a friend of his, Saul Blanche, who owned a small press at the time in New England   Vermont   so it was gratitude and they were also good friends

What was the occasion for the party to which they were going?

I have no information on that   an occasion?   no, I don't seem to have   an occasion, you say   the folder I have is labeled simply "The Party"   nothing about an occasion   that I can find

What were you doing in the car?

I wasn't in the car!   why would you think that I was in the car?

I have a photograph of the car taken as it passed under a streetlamp and it's obvious that the car has only   three   people in it, Mr. and Mrs. Henry and Mr. Lewis   would you like to see for yourself? take a look?

Did Guy make indecent advances to Sheila in the car?

Well, indecent   I don't know about indecent   I think that's the sort of thing that's in the eye of   all right, fine, the memo   it's rather sketchy   Mr. Lewis did a few   minor things   the memo never once uses   does it?   no   the word indecent, by the way Mr. Lewis did a few small things in a spirit of   fun, it seems   the memo isn't explicit but they seem to have been bawdy or   ribald? ribald   the memo, yes   at occasional stops for red lights Mr. Lewis touched Mrs. Henry on her breasts and on her   thighs and knees

and once put his hand   let me see now   put his hand under her
skirt   and here an interesting note states that he even told Mr.
Henry that his wife had the most beautiful legs he'd ever seen   I
think there was a lot of horseplay   no it doesn't say that but I'm
Mr. Lewis was quite   candid   it seems   I don't think a man an-
nounces really indecent, as you say, acts   advances, pardon me
that would seem to be it   Mr. Lewis touched Mrs. Henry a few times
and made a remark about her thighs   about her legs

     Was Guy Lewis married?

     He was indeed, for almost ten years, to a woman named
Joanne   I haven't got   yes I have   her maiden name was Harlan,
Joanne Harlan   all her friends called her Bunny   at this time
they'd been separated for   a while   I have a large envelope of
materials on Mrs. Lewis here, all sort of things   letters   diaries
a few drawings   and some   other things   not much of interest
just things I said   they're photographs that's all   of course, if you
wish, it's just that I don't understand you, you had no interest in the
photograph of Mrs. Henry nor the pair of photographs of the car but
you're interested in   I don't agree, I don't think you can prove anything from these photo   and what else?   odds and ends, knick-
knacks, souvenirs, private things that wouldn't make sense to anybody but   here's for instance a little amber glass ashtray that says
Welcome To Kansas City   and   here's a   book of matches from
Mama Gatto's Restaurant and a menu from   Imbriale's Clam House
    thank you   I still don't think that these photo   it's not my busi-
ness to think   all right   but to jump to conclusions doesn't seem

     Why were you invited to this party?

     I wasn't invited to the party   first you have me in the car, now
you have me at the party   soon you'll be saying that I was friendly
with everyone   look, I mind my business and do my best   I don't
get any pleasure out of all this   these folders and envelopes and
cartons full of old junk and stuff it's better to leave dead and buried
I can't imagine who'd want to know this, some sort of sick mind prod-
ding and poking into people's lives   this one, "The Party"   you can

look through it, every scrap and   what you'll find out is what I found
     Horace Rosette?   yes, but that's right here too   that doesn't
mean that I knew him or that I knew anything about any new book of
his   these are pieces and scraps   if you want to make connections
     go ahead   I certainly can't help it   I gathered these things to-
gether   believe me I don't get any pleasure out of all this   and
worked hard to get them in some kind of order because I knew that
you'd want   no I was not there   why would I be invited to Mr.
Rosette's?   I say it again   I didn't know these people   not at all
and when I say didn't know I don't mean know at a distance   I mean
I didn't know them   at all   what I know is what all this   all these
papers and things   know   if they know anything either
     Who was at the party?
     I'll just read the names off if that's   Horace Rosette, of course,
and you know that Mr. and Mrs. Henry and Guy Lewis were there
then there were Lucy Taylor, Lena Schmidt, Harlan Pungoe, Duke
Washington, Karen Ostrom, Buffie Tate, Vance Whitestone, Craig
Garf, Joanne Lewis, Leo Kaufman, Anne Kaufman, Ellen Kaufman,
Biff Page, Lee Jefferson, Chico Zeek, Anton Harley, Antonia Harley,
Page Moses, Baylor Freeq, Bart Kahane, Conchita Kahane, Lolita Kahane, Lincoln Gom, Roger Whytte-Blorenge, Dick Detective, April
Detective, Luba Checks, Sister Rose Zeppole, Ted Buckie-Moeller and
     that's it   that's the complete list
     It is?
     It is as far as I have it   I have another list here   of people
in the same folder   "The Party" folder?   but it must be a mistake
because they seem to be people who were involved with some film
that was being made   or being discussed   with the title   and
here's where the confusion comes in   the mistake   with the title
The Party   certainly I'll give you their names   but I don't think
they were all at the party necessarily even though they're in "The
Party" folder   fine   as long as all this is kept in mind so that things
don't get really confused   no   I don't have any idea why these
people should be in this folder   unless   you know the old saying

about it's a small world   unless some of the people at the party
"The Party" people   knew some of the people who were involved
with *The Party*   the film   yes I said I'd give you their   Tania
Crosse, Lorna Flambeaux, John Hicks, Jackson Towne, Léonie Au-
bois, Biggs Richard, Marcella Butler, Cecil Tyrell, Sol Blanc, Annette
Lorpailleur

What were Bart Kahane's motives in following Sheila into the
bathroom?

Motives is a strange word to use   I don't think that I'd use that
word   I have a few   three   accounts here but they're of necessity
secondhand, even thirdhand   it was a bathroom after all, it wasn't
exactly crowded with people was it?   the truth?   you talk as if I
was in the bathroom with   I understand   the consensus   that's
a good word, almost as good as motives   the consensus then   is
that Mr. Kahane's motives in following Mrs. Henry into the bathroom
were simply   he had to relieve himself and he had no idea that Mrs.
Henry was already in the bathroom   or that anybody at all was in
yes, she was when he walked in on her   that's why she was in the
bathroom   the what?   the scene?   what else would the scene
be?   it was embarrassing for both Mrs. Henry and Mr. Kahane   all
right, as clearly as I can, anybody who'd want to know all these things
is   I'm not judging anybody   Mr. Kahane entered the bathroom
because he had to   relieve himself   and he had no idea that
anybody   let alone a woman   let alone Mrs. Henry was   sitting
relieving herself   and Mr. Kahane saw her and she saw him and
there was a moment of   surprise   and embarrassment and then
Mr. Kahane   I don't know if they said anything   Mr. Kahane left
the bathroom as quickly as he had entered and a few moments later
Mrs. Henry emerged from   no there are no comments or reports or
anything else that say anything about laughter or remarks of any kind
being made by either   quickly means what it says   quickly
maybe a minute, less than a minute, a half a minute, a few seconds, a
split second, a fraction of a split   no I'm not being arrogant and
uncooperative   you're making me feel like a voyeur and believe me

I don't get any pleasure out of all this   anybody who'd want to
know all these things is pretty   what?   as modestly as possible, I'd
assume, from these statements   three, I said   I don't know how
they knew, all I did was get this stuff, these statements and diaries and
photographs   this material   together   Mrs. Kahane, Miss Lorpailleur, and Miss Jefferson   just a moment, let me see what   no,
not exactly that word   all right, not that word   I said modestly
because the statements are more or less in agreement as to it all being
an accident and embarrassing and   innocent in nature   of course
she knew Mr. Kahane   I'd have to check on that, it was   Mrs. Detective who introduced them   no, Mrs. Detective didn't make any
statement at all about this incident   no   nothing   yes, I have a
remark of Mrs. Detective's here but you said about this particular
bathroom incid   it's to the effect that Miss Lorpailleur told her that
Mr. Lewis had said in Miss Lorpailleur's hearing that he was really
angry with Mr. Kahane because Mr. Kahane had said that he had Mrs.
Henry's   an undergarment of Mrs. Henry's in   her panties   in
his pocket   why would it be odd for Mr. Lewis to be angry?   he was
a good friend of the Henrys   to whom?   Mr. Kahane said this
according to Mr. Lewis   to Sister Rose Zeppole   what?   I don't
know what time Miss Lorpailleur arrived   I don't know, but she and
Miss Ostrom shared an   that's right, as an editorial assistant   they
shared an apartment and probably arrived together   of course I'm
sure that Miss Lorpailleur was at the party!   the color of the?
black   anyone who'd want to   no not plain   trimmed with black
lace   my God, anyone who'd

Why did Lolita Kahane slap Conchita?

Now we're really getting involved in the past here   I've got to
go into a lot of old things here, diaries, letters   here's even a book
a novel about these things   a roman à   what do they call that?
roman à?   I can't remember   hold your horses!   I want to give
you the reasons and the background   no, I don't mistake the novel
for fact   I just mentioned the novel to show   *Isolate Flecks*
mentioned it to show you that these events were thought interesting

enough to write about in this roman à whatever it's called   all right,
here it   when Mr. Kahane was a young man he was in the Navy for
a while   four years, I think, but I don't know what importance that
four years   he married Conchita, a Mexican girl   couldn't speak
a word of English   then they got divorced and Mr. Kahane married
Lolita Schiller   I don't know, some machinist or lathe operator
by this time Mr. Kahane was beginning to get a reputation and beginning to sell pretty well   a sculptor   although he had been for many
years a painter   through the Gom Gallery   yes, Lincoln Gom, I
mentioned that he was at the party   Schiller? Richard   Richard
Schiller   I don't know, the latest information here is that he was last
seen in Flint   he may have paid him off as you put it   I don't know
    Mr. Kahane married Lolita Schiller and his career started to really
    as they say   take off   well, the testimony I have, which is all
anonymous so as to protect the innocent   that's a good one   the
innocent   I'm sorry, right, no comments   I thought that it might
help to relieve the boredom, I don't get any pleasure out of all this you
know   the testimony maintains that the present Mrs. Kahane, Lolita
Kahane, really set Mr. Kahane irrevocably   as they say   irrevocably
on the golden road to success   no I'm not being funny, what's the
matter with the phrase golden road to   all right   his career really
took off when a very important collector   Barnett Tete   bought a
large piece, *Gin City*   stainless steel and   wait a minute, some
kind of plastic   styrofoam   a piece that's now considered a mile-
stone in the movement   the movement called   I can't find it right
now but it's here somewhere   lyrical expressionism?   did you ever
hear of that?   abstract lyricism?   anyway, Mr. Tete bought the
piece and because he was such an important collector and connoisseur of the arts   especially contemporary art   Mr. Kahane's reputation was pretty well made and he began to   I'm getting to why
Mrs. Kahane slapped   the testimony   the anonymous testimony
says that Mr. Tete would never have bought the piece if Mrs. Kahane
hadn't   yes, the present Mrs. Kahane   Lolita Kahane   if she
hadn't   one says   if she hadn't granted certain   sexual favors

to Mr. Tete   another, if she hadn't prostituted herself to Mr. Tete
another, if she hadn't given herself to Mr. Tete   another   well, they
all go on in the same vein   they're really all the same, what's the use
of   all right, another says if she hadn't   blown Mr. Tete   another,
if she hadn't   gone down on Mr. Tete while Mr. Kahane was   my
God   in the next room fixing drinks   satisfied?   the slap, right
Conchita Kahane meanwhile had learned to speak perfect English
and went to work for Lincstone Productions as executive secretary to
Mr.   I didn't mention this earlier?   Lincstone Productions was
involved in developing properties   inexpensive properties   for
television   mostly television movies according to my reports from
here's a prospectus if you want to   you'll take my word for it?
that's a surprise   anyway, Mrs. Kahane, Conchita Kahane, became
executive secretary to Mr. Whitestone and was deeply involved in the
property called *The Party*   which is perhaps why she was at the
party at Mr. Rosette's   that's right   exactly   Lincoln Gom and
Vance Whitestone, Lincstone   so Mrs. Kahane   Conchita Kahane
was at the party with her boss and when she was introduced to the
present Mrs. Kahane she made a crack about her   indiscretions
supposed indiscretions   and the present Mrs. Kahane slapped her

   Is it possible that Conchita had learned of Lolita's indiscretions
with Mr. Tete through Bart?

   Supposed indiscretions   I said that these were mostly anonymous declarations   no, impossible   Mr. Kahane hadn't seen the
first Mrs. Kahane for many years and didn't even know that she was
working for Lincstone Productions   didn't even know she'd learned
to speak English for that matter   although a note here says that he
knew that she'd left Mexico   who?   Miss Ostrom, who was, I've
already told you, an ex-editorial assistant to Mr. Whitestone   when
he was in publishing, of course   when he went into partnership with
Mr. Gom he took Miss Ostrom along with him   no not as an editorial
assistant, as   an acquisitions   to be in charge of acquisitions   I
think that she may have acquired *The Party* property   or the rights
to the novel   is that the same thing?   the novel?   I'm sure I men-

tioned this   the novel was *La Soirée intime* by Léonie Aubois   yes
very modern   no I haven't read it   I can barely read French and
even if a translation were available I don't think that I'd care to read it
   this modern   so-called modern   fiction is confusing   you
can't keep anything straight   bad as life   yes, well a reader's report
says   this is a novel in which what we think of as reality is seen to
be, because of a fractured and multiple mirror image of self-reflec-
tive, as well as self-reflexive events, not at all the   the gist?   well
it seems to be a novel about a group of people who go to a party in
order to talk about making a film about the very party that they're
attending   you don't know after a while if what is going on at the
party is really going on at the party   or will go on in the movie that
they're supposed to be talking about making   and in the novel, the
movie that they're talking about making will also be called *La Soirée
intime*   it seems very self-conscious and   artificial   to me   for
whatever my opinion's
   Why did Bart Kahane tell Leo Kaufman that he had surprised
Anne Kaufman and Biff Page on Horace Rosette's bed?
   You'll pardon me if I say   I hope you'll forgive me if I tell you
that this is a ridiculous question?   I have this excerpt, the same one
that you've probably already seen   right here   and I was wondering if you'd be asking about anything that Miss Schmidt had   well
perhaps I don't have the same excerpt   but all my data point to the
fact that this was simply slander, this   is supposed to have come from
Miss Schmidt who supposedly made a tape recording of her views as
to what supposedly went on at the party   this and that   everything
from what was on the buffet table to the drinks available at the bar to
what books were discussed to various indiscretions and who said
what to whom   about whatever   acute observations   reasoned
opinions   sage judgments   no I wouldn't call it sarcasm, I don't
know of course Miss Schmidt   but I do have a thorough medical
report here   glance at it yourself   you'll see that it would have
been quite impossible for Miss Schmidt to have made a tape recording
because she was a deaf mute   beyond that   it's also the fact that

she had a very imperfect   command of the English language   so
that even had she managed to sputter and   stammer   or whatever
they   it's unlikely that she would have been able to make a statement
of any value   then there's all this other material, a matter of record,
public knowledge, what have you   I mean to say that Mr. and Mrs.
Kaufman, Anne Kaufman, had been divorced for years   so that why
Mr. Kahane would think that Mr. Kaufman would care if Mrs. Kaufman, the first Mrs. Kaufman, was in bed   my mistake   on the bed
with Mr. Page is beyond   what? impossible   it couldn't have been
the second Mrs. Kaufman   Ellen Kaufman   all my notes state that
she was seen all evening long circulating among the other guests and
never   disappeared for any length   of course I assume that she
went to the bathroom but that's not what I would call disappearing
now, if I may further squash   quash   this so-called eyewitness
indictment   no one states flatly in any of these reports that Mrs.
Kaufman, Anne Kaufman, was even at this party   the guest list?
that's a list that's all   but her name   as far as I can see   doesn't
come up again   and the clincher that contradicts this   these supposed   alleged   remarks by Miss Schmidt is that Mr. Page
although he might have been as you say   as Miss Schmidt allegedly
said   on the bed with either one Mrs. Kaufman or the other Mrs.
Kaufman he might as well have been there with a good book as the
saying goes because Mr. Page was a fa   homosexual   so the whole
thing is a   what do they call that? a tissue of lies   that somebody
came up with to denigrate people, these people supposedly involved
in   Mr. Page?   he did this and that   wrote theater and film reviews for a couple of weekly newspapers   the arty-radical-one-step-
ahead papers   you know   did some acting in little-theater groups
took courses in modern dance and poetry and that sort of thing
his living?   he was Mr. Zeek's   I don't know what you'd call it
a sort of housekeeper and secretary and valet   a sort of paid companion I suppose   Mr. Pungoe had got him the job   Mr. Pungoe?
he owned some sort of plant that manufactured some kind of   let
me check   oh yes   meat-cutting machines   no not an old friend

of Mr. Zeek's, they'd become friends when Mr. Zeek was involved in avant-garde films and Mr. Pungoe had patronized   been the patron for a film that Mr. Zeek had made   I'll check   *Hellions in Hosiery*   I have no idea, I have a clipping here   of course I'll read it   Annie Flammard brings new meaning to the tired words erotic imagination   from *Compost*   Annie Flammard?   I have nothing on her

What does the phrase "metallic constructions" mean?

Metallic constructions? I have no idea. Would you mind telling me where you got that one? I can't imagine what it is you're

Who was Annette Lorpailleur?

If I knew who Miss Lorpailleur was   she seems to be   at the center of everything   but the information on her is   what can I call it?   indecisive   inconclusive   all bits and pieces   she's not quite   there   one note says she taught school in France   some little town called either   Fanapa   or   Antoine   another says she wrote novels under the name Sylvie Lacruseille   here's a publicity photograph of Miss Lacruseille and if that's an author   I'll eat my hat   looks more like a starlet   and here's another photograph of Miss Lorpailleur   supposedly   you can see that Miss Lorpailleur is surely not Miss Lacruseille   then there's a brief entry on a page that looks as if it was torn from a diary that mentions that there was a scandal of some sort involving Miss Lorpailleur and Mr. Harley   Harley, yes   that's Mr. Anton Harley, not Mr. Harlan   there's no Mr. Harlan, there's a Mr. Harlan Pungoe   and you remember that I said that Mrs. Lewis's maiden name was Harlan   Joanne Harlan   but this is Mr. Harley   I don't know, some kind of a farmer or something   raised hogs or cows or whatever   yes, his wife's name was Antonia, but I gave you the list of guests   people at the   what?   that's all it says   some sort of scandal involving Miss Lorpailleur and Mr. Harley   at Mr. Marowitz's house   I'm sure I told you about Mr. Marowitz already   I know you're being patient as   Mr. Marowitz was Ellen Kaufman's father   the unknown   what do they call that?   the silent partner   in the Gom Gallery, according to these finan-

cial records   the one with the money   the real money   I don't
know exactly, some sort of businessman, quite wealthy   there's an
investigative report here that links him with Mr. Tete but it doesn't say
how or when or for how long they were associated   I don't know
whose diary   it just mentions some sort of scandalous behavior
the exact phrase   the verbatim phrase   Annette and Anton Harley's behavior was so shameless that no one had the courage to admit
that it was actually happening   that's all it says and it earlier mentions that this gathering was a Christmas party at Mr. Marowitz's
house   what?   I don't pretend to know why there's a similar scene
in *La Soirée intime*   I have these notes and records and files and
folders and diaries   and bits and pieces of reports and testimonies
and   God knows what else and   believe me I don't get any pleasure
out of all this   I'm doing it because I   for certain?   for certain,
Miss Lorpailleur shared an apartment with Miss Ostrom and was
somehow   I suppose   involved with *The Party*   I mean the movie
that was being   all right   she was it appears also a guest at the
party   and if she's not on the party list in the folder   I simply cannot
help that   if you think other people have better information
please   go ahead and ask them   ask anybody   you won't hurt
my feelings   far from it, I assure you   you certainly must realize
how hard it is to answer   to try and answer   these questions when
all I have are these   folders and files and   and all these papers
   But if what you've said about April Detective is true, how do
you explain these photographs of her?
   What I've said about is good   really good   I don't know
where you get the idea that I've said   anything   over and over
again   this is a bore   I've told you that I'm telling you what I've got
here in all these   Mrs. Detective had   for some years   been living
quietly in   New England with her husband   taking care of the
house, giving quiet parties   Vermont   I told you that earlier
giving quiet parties as I say   while Mr. Detective was working on a
novel   he'd always wanted to write a novel and   no I didn't say
Blackout   I said *Blackjack*   I don't know whether you realize it or

not but it's not easy trying to answer new questions and then go back
and answer   all over again   questions that I've already answered
trying to keep all these papers in some kind of reasonable order and
if I make a small mistake now and then   yes I'm sure it's *Blackjack*
yes, here's the dust jacket   *Blackjack* is right   Blanche Neige
Press, in a limited edition   Blanche Neige?   that's right, they also
published *Sheila Sleeping* and   or   *Lobster Lays*, Mr. Henry's
book   or books   I'm not certain   oh thanks, I'm glad that it's not
important   now that I've dropped this stuff all over the   yes, I am
a little piqued, as you put it   do this and do that and do the other
thing and then all of a sudden it's not important   anymore   yes,
Mr. Blanche was the   he was, so to speak, Blanche Neige Press
money?   he made enough I suppose to survive   led a simple life
the books were all   what do they call that?   they were all   letter-
press?   hand set   a labor of love   he had no regular assistants,
once in a while he'd put a   someone   up for a while   a few weeks
    or months   and they'd assist him in the work, he didn't have a
large operation, you understand   this was deluxe publishing for collectors   bibliophiles   well, Miss Crosse was there for a time
and Miss Flambeaux   Miss Butler   Mrs. Checks   no, I don't know
why they were all women   besides   they weren't all women because here   a letter shows that Mr. Harley would go over to Mr.
Blanche's house to help once in a   go over?   Mr. Harley was a
neighbor, he had a farm of some kind, I'm sure I've noted that   raised
chickens and pigs or something and lived about fifteen miles   no, I
never thought about it being a strange coincidence that they all lived
so close to each other   what exactly does all mean?   Mr. Harley
Mr. Blanche   and the Detectives is not exactly a crowd is it?   well
is it?   I know that you ask the   I'm not digressing   you're the one
who keeps elaborating these questions   about books and assistants
    and how come all these people lived so close to each   I haven't
forgotten your question   the simple truth is that, as I told you, I can't
explain these photographs of Mrs. Detective   I agree that they're
erotic   as far as pornographic   I wouldn't say that   we've been

through that, no, they weren't taken by Mr. Detective   because they were mailed to Mr. Detective at a time when he and Mrs. Detective were   temporarily separated and Mr. Detective had taken an apartment   the apartment's not important either   wonderful   well, if that is Mr. Harley it doesn't look like this other snapshot of him taken just a couple of years   apparently a couple of years before   I agree that this other woman appears to be Miss Lacruseille   but it's hard to tell because her face is   you can't really compare it to the publicity photo of her because the lighting is   use?   I don't know of any use that they were put to   Lorna Flambeaux?   her book was called *The Sweet* or *The Sweat of Love*   I can't quite make out this handwriting   and it was   it says here   illustrated with photographs but I don't think that evidence of any use   as you put it   of these photographs of Mrs. Detective   and other people   all right then pornographic   I'm perfectly willing to call a spade a spade   I just don't get any pleasure out   the book was also published by Blanche Neige Press   sure   I can give you a list but it's not, as far as I can tell, complete   let's see now   *Sheila Sleeping* and or *Lobster Lays* by Louis Henry   *The Orange Dress* by Sheila Henry   *Blackjack* by Richard Detective   I'm reading these right off the list   *The Sweet of Love*   it is *Sweet*   by Lorna Flambeaux   *Les Constructions métalliques* by Henri Kink   that's all I have   oh, I'd guess there were more books but this is far from complete   I think   no, he had no other income and these statements show that he probably couldn't have supported himself very well with the income from the press earlier?   earlier he had been involved with Mr. Tete and Mr. Pungoe in some sort of real estate   real estate   thing   partly real estate and there are legal papers here   I can't understand a word of them about some legal   action or suit concerning   let me see   concerning some sort of   suit or action concerning   it's something about   forgeries of   prints   the defendants were Mr. Blanche Mr. Tete   Mr. Harley   and   Mr. Gom   I imagine   yes   that you can make a lot of money that way   yes   enough to buy a house and land almost anywhere   yes   Vermont included   Sol Blanc?

he was one of the people   I mentioned him   involved with *The Party* project   this report says that he was   a photographer   and that he had been engaged for a time to   Miss Crosse who was don't tell me I beat you to it?   Miss Crosse was a photographer too fashion photography   what?   it doesn't say but I suppose that she could have done   any kind of photography   there's nothing here but certainly she could have known Mrs. Detective but I don't see that that   implies anything   anybody can know anybody   right? right?

Do I understand you to mean that Joanne Lewis—Bunny—had known Harlan Pungoe long before she met Guy?

That's what everything seems to point to   but I don't know why you're making a federal case out of it   she was still single and had a perfect right to do whatever she   in some small town   Boonton   or   Katydid Glade   ashamed of her father?   I don't think so   yes a high school teacher   automotive trades   but Bunny had what they call a good relationship   no, not my tired phrase   as you put it   I'm reading it right off this sheet   I don't know what the significance of the Indian corn being hung up by Mrs. Lewis's mother has to   there's nothing here about anything like Indian corn   yes she'd had some affairs   yes   one was with a young English novelist

I don't know what Mr. Ward's reaction to his daughter's taking up, as you say, with Mr. Lewis   as I said   she was single and   Mr. Ward?   Mrs. Lewis's father of course   you remember him   the automotive trades   Ward?   yes   Mrs. Lewis's maiden name was Joanne Ward   I've already   Harlan?   no   not Harlan   you're thinking about Mr. Pungoe   I said Joanne Harlan?   impossible it's right here   I jotted   Joanne   Joanne   well   I can't imagine why I said Harlan   it's definitely Ward   Joanne Ward   no I'm not trying to confuse you   God knows that I'm the one who's confused with this one and that one and ex-wives and ex-husbands and everything else that I   protect people?   that's really   that's really an insulting remark after I've done my best to   Mr. Pungoe, yes came between the English novelist and Mr. Lewis   but it was brief

and more like a   friendship   than anything else   he was quite a
bit older than   friendship is what I said   yes   I called her Harlan
because her relationship with Mr. Pungoe was what?   an indelible
experience?   indelible is quite a mouthful   after all   Mrs. Lewis
was not exactly Bo-Peep when she met Mr. Pungoe   and even though
he was a mature and   experienced man   she wouldn't exactly be
so impressed by this brief   relationship   so as for it to be indel
I don't think strange tastes could be applied to Mr.   what book?
now this is the sort of thing that it's unlikely I can find in   yes   I
said a large envelope but that doesn't mean that everything in the
world will necessarily be in the envel   but   well   so it is   how
lucky we are, now we can really get to the bottom of this mysterious
and   profound   and really   sinister   well I'm tired of your
insinuations   particularly when I have very little choice   I'd be
happy if you talked to somebody who knew these people firsthand
believe me   I don't get any pleasure out   all right so I've said that
already   it seems to me that I can't say it too often because your
insinuations are really getting to   the book?   the title isn't given,
it only says   in its entirety   she told Guy about it once and he
started to read to her from Stekel   I don't have any idea what she
might have   these photographs   again?   I told you that I don't
think you can prove a thing from these   I say that because it's obvious to me that these are posed   some sort of a   joke   all right
that's not the right word   I admit   maybe a   or maybe this was a
modeling job   something like that   Mrs. Lewis had to eat   as
they say   and you know those bizarre fashion photographs that they
     bizarre   you know what I mean   bizarre   strange   a sug-
gestion of   perversion   fetishism   bondage   whatever they
think is   I mean maybe she was simply making a few dollars   it's
an adobe house but what's wrong with that?   you see all kinds of
things   locations   adobe houses and townhouses and penthouses
     lawns and construction sites   bridges and vacant lots the subway
     even art galleries and saloons   they use any damn stupid back-
ground that they   the man?   could be anybody at all   some model

or   some sort of model   I think he looks very much like a model,
yes   I can't give you any idea at all why Mr. Lewis would read from
Hegel to   Stekel   from Stekel to Mrs. Lewis   I never heard of
Stekel   I don't know if they met before Mr. Pungoe got involved with
Mr. Zeek   no I've never seen it and I've never even seen a picture of
      this other woman is Annie Flammard?   absolutely   there's no
doubt that she's Miss Lacruseille or   as they say   her double   do
I find what else odd?   no I don't think there's anything else particularly odd   it's a still   obviously   from a movie   I suppose it's
Hellions in Hosiery but I wouldn't be able   you don't mean that?
how am I supposed to know exactly what you're driving   oh   yes
it looks like the same adobe house but it seems to me that all adobe
houses look   where in both of them?   yes I see   it's a drawing
on the wall   it's the same drawing   all right   it is odd but then
it's very easy to make all kinds of assumptions about all kinds of things
when you don't have all the information   there is probably a perfectly good   a perfectly plausible reason as to why   Baylor Freeq?

I mentioned him when I told you   I didn't mention him?   it
seems as if I did but anyhow   he was Miss Flammard's co-star in
Hellions in Hosiery   just a moment, I have to find   Mr. Freeq was
an actor who worked in small experimental theaters and experimental repertory groups   had been in a number of plays   some of
them?   some of them were   this can't be right   it says that he
was in *The Party*   a one-act play by Craig Garf   that can't be right
unless   I mean it's too strange a coincidence   that's what it says
The Party   and the other vehicles   I love that word   it always
makes me think of a bunch of actors   I'm sorry   I don't mean to
waste time   Mr. Freeq   was also in *Ten Eyck Walk* and *The Caliph*
and *Black Ladder*   it was a stage name   his real name was   just
a   his real name was Barry Gatto   no there's no mention of him
having anything to do with Lincstone Productions or *The Party*   the
movie   the projected movie I   all right, I just wanted to keep things
as straight as   Mr. Henry?   yes   he knew Mr. Henry, not very
well   they had a kind of   I don't know   business arrangement

having to do with Mr. Henry's car   Mr. Freeq was paying off Mr.
Henry's car for him   there's no clue here as to why so I don't know
they were friends   maybe they had come to some sort of arrangement   Mr. Freeq was an old friend of Mrs.   Mr. and Mrs. Henry
he'd known the Henrys years before when Mr. Henry was a graduate
student   there was some sort of help he'd given Mr. Henry especially
       something that could have been a tragic   yes he'd helped both of
them   Mrs. Henry tried to   she put her head in the oven because
she was so unhappy at being   feeling   left out of her husband's
Mr. Freeq had been a very good friend at the time   well, he'd found
her   so I imagine that Mr. Henry felt that he owed   and Mrs. Henry
too of course   they felt that they owed him a great deal and   I don't
know why he'd pay off his car if it was Mr. Henry who was indebted to
       what?   more than meets the eye?   oh please, this is just   yes
I am tired   sick and tired   maybe Mrs. Henry   the Henrys
had somehow given Mr. Freeq more than he expected and he found
himself in debt then   to them   I don't know what Mrs. Henry
the Henrys gave him   I said maybe gave him   yes, Mr. Freeq knew
Mrs. Lewis when she was still Miss Har   Miss Ward   as a matter
of fact she first met Mr. Lewis at a little café that Mr. Freeq had a part
interest in   Mama Gatto's   just a name, there was no Mama Gatto
       it was apparently a kind of private joke because only a few people
knew that Mr. Freeq's real name was   right   it says that it closed
within a year or so   fire violations or health violations about
something about storing   paints and dyes   no   for fine-arts use
       storing them   in the basement   I have no idea why he would
store such things in   a passing acquaintance with Mr. Tete, yes
through Mr. Kahane who knew the Henrys   no there's no record of
legally fighting   anything   he closed the café and that was   I
don't know what happened to the materials in the base   what?
well, that would depend, wouldn't it, on whether or not Miss Lorpailleur was   I mean   yes   Mr. Freeq knew Miss Lorpailleur only if
Miss Lorpailleur was also Miss Lacruseille   which I doubt because
of the photographs that we looked at a   and whether then Miss La-

cruseille was also or actually Miss Flammard   which might be so
because this still from the movie looks like the   you get what I mean?

he knew Miss Flammard whoever she was   of course   because
he was her co-star in   right   I don't think that he knew Mr. Pungoe

despite the fact that Mr. Pungoe was the   what do they call   the
angel   he was the angel for *Hellions in*   what?   because he knew
Mrs. Lewis and Mrs. Lewis knew Mr. Pungoe it doesn't follow that
people can know people who know people that they don't know, you
know what I   what? I don't have any record of that as far as I can see

except for one brief note that you can take   again   with a grain
of salt because it is supposedly by Miss Schmidt who as we know
fine, for what it's worth   a good way to put it   it states that Mr.
Pungoe took Mrs. Lewis to one of the shooting locations   one afternoon   *Hellions in Hosiery*!   what other film could I be talking
about?   *The Party* wasn't a film, it was a one-act   you've confused
it yourself with the film that was just being talked about at the party
I'm expected to keep everything straight when you   with your information as well as mine   and God knows who else has told you
whatever comes into their heads   you have as much trouble as I
these papers and files and ex-whatevers and friendships and   who
knows exactly when this   I mean it's not as if all this is dated   and
in order   no wonder that   I'm just getting it off my chest   let's go
on   by all means

What did April Detective see when she entered Mr. Rosette's
study?

Mrs. Detective has written   in passing   in a letter to Mr.
Kahane about that   it's a very   distraught   letter that falls
maybe   in the category of the woman scorned   I suppose jealous
it seems to me accusatory   of Mr. Kahane   exactly?   your behavior was so shameless that I didn't have the courage to admit to
myself that what I saw was actually happening   I don't know what
she means by behavior   after the bathroom?   I don't know if this
was after or before   it could well have been compromising   certainly   that I can't tell you   but it's fairly obvious that it was   that

Mrs. Detective and Mrs. Kahane   Lolita Kahane   were very good
friends and perhaps Mrs. Detective felt that it was   unwise   for
Mr. Kahane to be alone with Mrs. Henry because of what it might have
looked like to the other guests   Mr. Rosette?   most of the evening
he was at the   tending bar   he enjoyed tending bar when he gave
a party even though   I was about to say   even though he had a
bartender who was   I imagine   perfectly competent   Mr. Towne
I believe   I know nothing about him except that Mr. Rosette often
employed him to tend   he may have been living with Mr. Rosette at
the time, I don't know   no I didn't know that he'd reviewed *The Orange Dress*   qualifications? do you need qualifications to review a
book?   it seems to me that any fool who can write   you'll pardon
the expression   English can review a   also in *Compost?*   isn't
that   sinister and mysterious, isn't that really   well you have this
faculty?   faculty   this faculty for making all of this   these things
into a kind of complicated web of   certainly Mr. Rosette could
have gone into his study, after all it was his study and it certainly
doesn't seem out of the ordinary for him to   with Mrs. Detective?
he may well have   perhaps for some privacy to talk about Mr. Detective's novel, *Blackjack*   which he wanted very badly to use   to
take some sections or chapters from for an anthology that he was   I
told you that he was an editor and an anthologist   well-known
oh many books   just a minute, some of the better known   some of
them   used in freshman English courses in a lot of   here it is
Tableaux Vivants: Selected Poems of Pamela Ann Clairwil   Mr. Rosette edited and introduced that   also *Gusty*   I mean *Gutsy*
Gutsy Ghetto Tales   and the best-known   an anthology
Bridges: Poets Express Their Love   yes he made a very good living
he also acted as a kind of   literary consultant   did editing and
proofreading and wrote jacket   what do they call that?   blurbs?
no   jacket copy   and reader's reports for various publishers
and did essays and reviews as well   all in all a   man of letters
no I'm not jok   Mrs. Detective instead of Mr. Detective?   that's a
good question to which I don't have the   I see you're waving those

photographs again in my   we've been through this before and I ad-
mitted that they're a little   that they're   risqué   we seem to be
drowning in photographs   as if a photograph could tell us   I am
looking   well if you say that this is Mr. Rosette's couch in Mr. Rosette's study then you know better than I do and if you know better
than I do then aren't we wasting our   he might well have taken the
photographs   he also might well have sent them to Mr. Detective
but for what reason I   yes I told you that the Detectives knew Mr.
Blanche   that they were neighbors in Ver   Mr. Rosette wanted to
get in on the what?   the print   scheme?   I'm not following you
I told you that that involved   it was never   what's the word?
litigated?   prosecuted?   there was a lack of evidence that
again?   again   Mr. Blanche   Mr. Tete   Mr. Harley   Mr. Gom
Mr. Detective might well have known something about it because he
was   as I said and said and said   a neighbor of Mr. Blanche's and
Mr. Blanche was his publisher so there was a good possibility that he'd
heard something about it   you know small communities   the pictures might have been a kind of blackjack?   I mean blackmail?
so that Mr. Detective would what?   his friendship with Mr. Blanche
to   that seems to me a lot of trouble to go to for a well-off man who
was profitably involved in the arts   and letters   and   no it's not
incomprehensible   it just seems to me to be   you're once again
digressing, not I   I told you about Mrs. Detective's letter to Mr. Kahane and that seems to me to be clear enough   I mean exactly that
clear enough   she doesn't mention in the letter anything about what
she saw in Mr. Rosette's study   there's one small note on the back of
an envelope here   I don't know who wrote it   it says   April pale
and trembling after seeing Sheila doing B   it seems to me the pale
and trembling is pretty   overwrought   purple   doesn't it to you?

I wouldn't know who   or what   B is   depositions?   that's a
pretty fancy word for what people thought they saw   or knew   but
if that's what you want to call them   I do have some other   depositions   here   here's one from Miss Schmidt   and anything she
says is as I've already told you to be taken with a grain   a very large

grain of   she says that Mrs. Henry was performing a sex act with Mr. Kahane   here's one from   this can't be be right   it's supposedly made by Miss Lacruseille   impossible   that says that   this is very vulgar indeed   verbatim?   verbatim then   Sheila was deliriously sucking Bart Kahane's   this is really too much, it might be a description of a scene from *Hell*   a hell of a filthy blue movie   I'll read it yes   God, anyone who'd want to know this stuff is really   Sheila was deliriously sucking Bart Kahane's   my God   enormous rigid cock   you know I don't mind giving you the gist of this garbage but when you get something filthy supposedly said by someone who wasn't even at   as far as I know from the list   wasn't even at   the party then I really feel as if things are going   one more yes   there's one more   this is a statement by Mr. Rosette   so it says   I tried to shield Mrs. Detective from the surprising and disgusting scene that greeted our eyes as we entered my study, but I was too late and fear that she saw every detail of the licentious behavior of this, what word can I use? this shameless couple   no   he nowhere mentions what couple it is   so much for your   depositions   I don't think at all that it follows that the bathroom incident was arranged   as you say after all you'll remember   speaking of depositions   that I gave you the deposition of Mrs. Kahane and the deposition of Miss Jefferson and the deposition of Miss Lorpailleur   Mrs. Henry's panties?   just a minute   I'm confused here   let me dig out   oh yes you'll remember that that was something that Mrs. Detective said that Miss Lorpailleur told her and that Miss Lorpailleur had overheard Mr. Lewis saying that he had been told this by Mr. Kahane   I mean   this was hearsay   in spades   Miss Jefferson?   she'd been an editorial assistant to Mr. Whitestone before he and Mr. Gom became partners in Lincstone Pro   yes she was an editorial assistant along with Miss Ostrom   how do I know?   I don't know how many assistants a senior editor needs but I imagine a   well whether I said so or not he was a senior editor   at Crescent and Chattaway   he may have had three or four or ten assistants   it doesn't seem to me to   thank you

I'd be delighted to continue   Miss Jefferson didn't go with Miss

Ostrom and Mrs. Kahane, Conchita Kahane   to Lincstone   she
opened a little boutique with Lucy Taylor   very chic and expensive
it's right here   Lorzu Fashions   Lorzu Fashions for the Woman of
Punctilious Dash is what their card says   Lorzu?   that's lor from
Taylor and zu from ZuZu   which was Miss Jefferson's nickname
Miss Taylor?   she'd been a sweetheart of Mr. Lewis's   an old flame
as they say   no not his childhood sweetheart   I think that's carrying mockery and cynicism a little   you accuse me of making cracks
about this and   as a matter of fact he did have a childhood sweetheart   Ann Taylor Redding   no I don't think they were sisters,
Taylor is a name like Smith or Brown isn't it?   there's a million Taylors   you think that there are too many coincidences?   what can I
say?   you get ten or twenty or   fifty people who know each other
and you're bound to get coincidences   and all sorts of odd   what's
the word I'm looking for?   alliances   no not alliances though alliances is all right but   I can't seem to   say   call them   config-
urations   it seems to me that with your questions and doubts and
going back over the same ground you're complicating things more
than   it is a maze   I agree   but I'm trying to give you what I have
    as objectively and cogently as   well all right   an occasional
opinion but based on materials that I   I have no interest in protecting anyone   why would I want to   what?   lies?   look I can give
you all this   all these papers   everything   I don't get any pleasure
out of this   as I suggested   ask somebody else   somebody who
personally knew these people   it's all right with   my God   I
mention two Taylors and immediately it's a significant   it's significant   you wouldn't think this was strange if you read it in a novel
like the one by Mademoiselle Aubois   *La Soirée intime*   where
you don't know if what's happening is happening or   something
which reminds you of *The Party*? oh   it reminds you of the *party*
the question   right   which was?   all right, to answer as precisely
as possible   from the evidence to hand   the depositions   Mrs.
Detective saw   in Mr. Rosette's study   Mrs. Henry performing a
sexual act   fellatio   on Mr. Kahane   that's all you wanted to

know?   fine   then why you got into all the other things I'll never
of course   let's continue   we've only been here about a hundred
years   at this rate

      Tell me some more about Annette Lorpailleur—for instance,
what did she do at this party?

      Well as I said before, she seems to be at the core of so many
things   and nobody knew precisely where she came from   Ga-
poine or something   Fagapa   it's spelled so many different   God
knows what the name of   yes I understand that you want details of
the party   I'm coming to   you have to realize that she seemed to
be everywhere   and that the reports on her are   to say the least
contradictory   I suppose I can start any   fine   just as the material is arranged   arranged is a great word to use for this   this
all right   to start she was involved in some kind of quarrel with Mr.
Whitestone as well as a real shouting match with Mademoiselle Aubois but for   I think   yes   different reasons but they had something to do with each other   probably   apparently she was doing
some pretty heavy   petting   in full view of   with Miss Ostrom
and Mr. Whitestone somehow objected and there was   as I say
there was a quarrel about   no I don't know anything about Miss
Ostrom and Mr. White   the acquisitions coordinator or something
other than that I   they indeed shared an apartment   she may have
  they may have been lesbians   I have no idea about that   Mademoiselle Aubois?   that was perhaps more serious since it had to
do with something   I don't know what happened first   you said to
reel this goss   this stuff off as   Mademoiselle Aubois?   there's
no evidence as to her sexual preferences and   I am trying to tell you
about   Miss Lorpailleur is said to have been trying to persuade Mr.
Whitestone to give her a part in *The Party* since Lincstone was   you
know all this   fine   as long as you know it God forbid that I should
repeat any   what?   if I said that Miss Ostrom was involved in ac-
quiring the rights to *The Party*   or to *La Soirée intime* precisely
then that's what I said but I   oh   you mean if Miss Ostrom was the
one in charge of this deal for Lincstone then Miss Lorpailleur   it's

rather crude and obvious   isn't it?   oh   I see   why the sudden
passion when she and Miss Ostrom were always together as   oh
you mean   I see what you're driving at   for the benefit of Mr.
Whitestone   so that he would maybe give her   if she'd stop with
Miss Ostrom   the part   that would presuppose   of course I can
see the possibility of Mr. Whitestone and Miss Ostrom being lovers
and if not then   then I don't know why he was so upset   maybe he
thought that it wasn't too good for the Lincstone image for its acquisitions   person   to be writhing around with her skirt all up around
her   I don't know what Mr. Whitestone said about any part for Miss
Lorpailleur   no I didn't say that Miss Flammard was at the party
only that Mr.   Mr.   who the hell was it now?   Mr. Freeq had been
her co-star   right   Miss Lorpailleur had no acting experience but
she had a kind of   obscure   background as I've   I told you about
the novelist   business   Lacruseille?   I did   well God knows
she may well have had acting experience   I never thought of that
yes   she might well have been Miss Flammard   which would
make her Miss Lorpailleur as well as Miss Lacruseille and Miss Flammard and a lesbian a novelist an actress   maybe she was also a maid
a nurse a nun a policewoman a corporation executive a doctor   fine!
     she may well have been Annie Flammard   except that you seem
to be forgetting the photographs that   faked?   fine   faked
whatever you say   Mademoiselle Aubois?   at some point Mademoiselle Aubois and Miss Lorpailleur got into a terrible quarrel
maybe because Miss Ostrom's skirt was up   I'm sorry   I'm thinking of Mr. Whitestone   pretty soon I won't know what I'm   they
had a terrible quarrel because Miss Lorpailleur claimed that *La Soirée intime* was a case of plagiary   that Mademoiselle Aubois had
read a manuscript of Miss Lorpailleur's only it was signed by Miss
Lacruseille   it's so stated   and stolen almost everything from it for
her own book   I don't know anything about the truth of this   only
that there are fragments here from I guess letters   about publishing
a novel by a Miss Lacruseille   Sylvie Lacruseille   from Crescent
and Chattaway   yes as a matter of fact   signed by Mr. Whitestone

some five years ago   or is it?   I can't tell, it might be   fifteen or
twenty-five?   what?   Miss Ostrom may well have been employed
at the time by Crescent and Chattaway but I don't think there's anything on it   no   not as far as I   it was titled   let me see   it
was going to have the English title of *Mouth of Steel*, in French it was
La Bouche métallique   no, apparently it wasn't published as *Mouth
of Steel*   and it wasn't published as   it wasn't published in France
either   it wasn't published period   doesn't say a thing about any
reason, just that the deal was off   yes there were other incidents
involving Miss Lorpailleur   here's another set of memos stapled together   how official   about Miss Lorpailleur approaching Mr. Gom
about a part in *The Party* and   depending on what you want to believe   if anything   all this seems as if it comes out of   talk about
fiction   out of a novel by some obsessed   all right   Miss Lorpailleur, as I said, and Mr. Gom   she either   offered him Miss Ostrom   or as I say   depending on what you want to   I know that
you can   or Miss Lorpailleur suggested that she had certain
records and other proofs   concerning Mr. Gom's finances   the
monies that had enabled him to go into partnership with Mr. Whitestone while still holding on to the gallery   I'm getting to   the records had to do with certain large amounts of money that came from
Mr. Gom's involvement with the   situation?   whatever   the business with the faked   the forged prints that I mentioned earlier?
I'm getting to that   if you'll just take it   I'm getting there   Miss
Lorpailleur allegedly told Mr. Gom that she knew all about his financial dealings because of Mr. Marowitz who was   you'll remember
the money man   what a disgusting phrase   the money behind the
Gom Gallery, so she knew all about the money that had been made
through the sale of the prints and how much had come to Mr. Gom
how?   well that's an interesting question   for a change   because
Miss Lorpailleur swears up and down in about half a dozen different
places   here, see?   and here   and here   and here   she swears
that it wasn't true, but Mr. Marowitz and Mr. Harley and Mrs. Kaufman
    Ellen Kaufman   and Mr. Kaufman   all swore on a stack of bibles

as they say   that Miss Lorpailleur was Mr. Marowitz's maid   and
for some time   it's really too much   isn't it?   what do I mean? I
mean   a French maid!   my God   it's just like that Annie Flammard movie, *Silk Thighs*   what?   I never implied that I never saw
a film starring Miss Flammard   I distinctly remember saying that I
never saw *Hellions*   fine, let's let it pass   and also   here it is
also   in addition to this sworn testimony, if that's what it is   sworn
or testimony   there's an interesting note that says   an anonymous
note   that says   that Miss Lorpailleur wasn't really Mr. Marowitz's
maid   only that she was his friend   it says friend   someone who
would come and visit regularly and dress up for him like a maid
yes, this little piece of notepad paper   the little note in red ink at the
bottom is a little list   it says   French maid   nurse   nun
policewoman   corporation executrix   doctor   what?   yes of
course I'm thinking what you're   it's a list of roles   that somebody
wanted somebody to play for   or that somebody played for   maybe
Mr. Marowitz   maybe not   I don't know   she may well have been
    yes   the maid   so to speak   when she was involved   alleg-
edly   in the alleged scandalous behavior with Mr. Harley but if you'll
recall that was mentioned briefly in a diary entry and   I hold no
brief, as you put it, for anybody   can't we get off this party?   you
talk as if you've never been to a party   I mean any party   at any
party the things that are liable to go on   the old friends and new
friends and husbands and wives and exes and lovers and the unspoken
    I'm not trying to educate anybody   yes, yes, and yes   again
Miss Lorpailleur   or Lacruseille or Flammard   whoever she was
    whatever her name   might have been a maid at the time of the
incident with Mr. Harley   or the nun   how should I know?   what?
    why?   because it's on the list here   I happened to think of a nun,
I could just as well have thought of   Sister Rose Zeppole was
according to this and that and the other thing   all these papers and
I'm sick of this, I might as well just make it all   invent the whole
thing since whatever I tell you you insinuate that   I was about to say
that   according to these unimpeachable sources   these sources

that glow with golden shining truth, Sister   I wouldn't call it sneer-
ing   Sister Rose Zeppole was a real nun   about thirty-two according to these unim   all that this brief note says   and oddly enough
or maybe not oddly at all   this note is in the folder labeled *The Party*
     the film   right   not "The Party" folder with the list of   right
of course I told you that *The Party*   the film   has a folder all to
itself?   more like a small carton in fact   I'm getting on with it
the note says that Miss Lorpailleur spoke for about ten minutes to Sister Rose Zeppole and that Sister Rose Zeppole   I can't quite make it
out   she either blushed or flushed   I grant you that it's strange that
a nun should be involved with such a group of   I don't know how or
why   there's absolutely nothing about   well there is one little
scrawl here on the report on the Detectives   it seems that   read
it?   all right   it reads   Sister Rose of great help to D.D. in marital
troubles in spirit of SIS   not sis, it's all in capitals   S I S   no, that's
all   I have no idea   I wouldn't even attempt to venture a guess
pretty?   I suppose you could call her pretty   here's a snapshot
taken of her when she was a   what do they call that?   an apprentice
nun?   a novice, right   I'd say about twenty or twenty-one   no I
don't think she looks like Mrs. Detective, as a matter of fact   nothing
     nothing   I was only going to say that she looks a little bit like Miss
Lorpailleur but in the light of the conversation that Miss Lorpailleur
had with her it can't be possible can it?   can it?   I know that you
ask the

     Can you give me a brief synopsis of *La Bouche métallique* or
Mouth of Steel?

     Certainly   I have a translator's   or reader's   or something
report right here   are we actually off this party?   here's the   O.K.
     La Bouche métallique is   it's signed   Roger Whytte-Blorenge
La Bouche métallique is an ingenious novel of worlds within worlds
it concerns a young man, Antoine, whose best friend, Octave, is asking
him persistent questions about a dinner party that Antoine has not
only not attended but most of whose guests he has never met   Antoine soon discovers that Octave is trying to find out whether his wife,

Roberte, who is Antoine's lover and who was a guest at the dinner party, permitted herself to be seduced by an officer of the Guards Antoine gallantly attempts to protect Roberte's reputation by inventing the incidents of the dinner party   he decides that painting too innocent or ingenuous a picture of Roberte will only serve further to excite Octave's suspicions, and so tells him that Roberte was accidentally instrumental in saving the honor of her old school friend, Jeannette, by stumbling into the bathroom at precisely the moment at which   what?   yes   stumbling into the bathroom but I don't think that it means that she actually stumbled but that   if you'll let me go on   fine   at precisely the moment at which the officer of the Guards and Jeannette were about to satisfy their carnal desires   so you see he means stumbled on   fine   carnal desires   Antoine further tells Octave that Roberte confided to him that she was shocked at Jeannette's licentiousness, but not surprised by it, because her husband, unlike Octave, had for years been cold and inattentive toward her   at this moment Roberte enters the room carrying a book and tells Octave and Antoine that she has just finished it   it is, she says, a fascinating new novel set at a dinner party during the course of which a beautiful young wife whose husband is out of town on business is tempted to be unfaithful to him with a handsome actor   just at the moment when she feels herself yielding she remembers her husband's kindness, wisdom, and quiet, strong love and she rejects temptation   the actor then reveals that he has been hired by her husband to test her chastity at which moment the husband himself steps out of the room into which the actor was about to lead the young wife   Roberte then smiles at Octave and kisses him tenderly, meanwhile looking knowingly and lecherously at Antoine, who is leafing through the novel which is in reality an erotic *récit* entitled *La Soirée intime*   Miss Lacruseille's novel is witty, dry, delicately ironic, and reverberant with suggestion   all in all a wonderfully controlled piece of writing   that's it   the entire report   I don't know if Miss Aubois had got hold of the manuscript or if she did whether or not she plagiarized it or   of course there are a number of similarities given

the information we have on the novels   but I haven't read either of
well yes   the title of the novel in Miss Lacruseille's   Miss Lorpailleur's novel   that's suspicious

Why did John Hicks visit Horace Rosette some time after the
party had broken up?

John   Hicks?   I don't think I mentioned any John   oh I
see   yes, he's in *The Party*   the movie   group   if that's what
you want to call it   I don't know why   I don't have anything of any
value at   maybe he was just a friend   even Horace Rosette had
friends I'm sure   I don't mean even   I mean that anybody has
friends that other people might not know anything ab   two little
lines that's all   one says   this must be somebody's idea of a joke
it says that he was some sort of city official   the Buildings Department   well I think it's a joke   or a mistake because what would a
city   a Buildings official be doing with people who were all involved
    more or less   with the arts   theater and film and what have
you?   yes that's all it says, some sort of city official involved with
in   the Buildings   the other line?   just as brief   it says that he
was a recent acquaintance of Mrs. Henry   that's all   no, not what
kind of an acquaintance   no, Mr. Henry isn't mentioned   no   it
doesn't say a word about this Mr.   Mr. Hicks   knowing Mr. Tete or
Mr. Pungoe   look for your   me?   I don't have any opinion, as I
told you, I   well if you want to call that an opinion but   to me   it
seems obvious that a man involved in real   ordinary   work   you
know   a regular nine to five job   would seem out of place with
people like the people involved with *The Party*   the film   and the
party itself   don't you think so?   don't you?   again   a city official in the Buildings Department   that's one   two   a recent acquaintance of Mrs. Henry   how should I know how he managed to
meet Mrs. Henry?   my God   Mrs. Henry probably met a million
where?   what do you mean where?   anywhere, everywhere, how
the   I am tired and confused, if you'd just stick with one line of   I
don't know why Mr. Hicks went to see Mr. Rosette   Mr. Rosette may
have been alone   why wouldn't he be alone if the party was over?

look at what?   this?   of course I can   it shows four men sitting
around a table, one is looking at a   loose-leaf book?   one is looking
at the one who is looking at the loose-leaf   one is smoking a   you
asked me what it   on the back?   yes   four names   Rosette,
Pungoe, Tete, Hicks   so?   so Mr. Hicks did know Mr. Pungoe and
Mr. Tete   maybe   I still don't know what he was doing at   under
the lamp?   under what lamp?   I see   it   it looks like it could
be   anything   it looks like a woman's   things   a scarf I think
and   and   could be anything   I suppose   a scarf and
under   underthings   under   a slip and   I guess panties   yes,
black   no, with black lace   why anyone would want to   I don't
know!   they could be Mrs. Henry's and they could be the Queen of
Sheba's   how should I know whose   or why?   what?   wait a
minute   you're the one who said that the party had broken up
well, whether you're interested or not you said that the   no I can't
imagine a woman forgetting them   unless she was   well, drunk
or maybe for a prank?   I take it back, you're right   it's not much of
a   all right   let's assume that they're Mrs. Henry's   now what?
what?   I still don't know what Mr. Hicks was doing at Mr. Rosette's
God knows, Mrs. Henry's   assuming they're Mrs. Henry's things
don't answer the question   neither does this photograph   does it?

I mean, what do you think this photograph has in it to   right   I
do the answering   but I can't hear   can I?   what a photograph
is saying   I mean   what these men are saying   can we get off the
Mr. Hicks business for now?

And what did Lolita have to say to Sheila on the telephone?

The transcription of the tape is   spotty   a lot of blank spaces,
apparently the tape was   it's unintelligible in a lot of   in effect,
Mrs. Kahane told Mrs. Henry that her husband   Mr. Kahane that is
her husband had confessed all   a little melodramatic I'd say,
wouldn't you agree?   you wouldn't agree   I thought you shook
your   pardon me   it doesn't have any information about what it
all means, no   there's a deletion noted   no I don't think anybody,
as you say, did it   I told you that the tape apparently was faulty

yes there's some more   Mrs. Kahane insisted   it seems over and
over again   seems?   all right, she did insist   over and over again
that Mrs. Henry do the same with Mr. Henry   right   the same
meaning that Mrs. Henry should tell Mr. Henry what she did with Mr.
Kahane   if you will   yes   confess all   no there's no mention
here of where   if it was true, of course it would have had to be   I
suppose   at the party   I don't know   the bathroom   or the study
    I don't know why you're making a mountain out of a molehill   I
don't care what I said!   it's not what I said anyway   it's what this
and this   this and this   these   goddamned papers and files and
God knows what else   I'm so confused with who did what and with
whom   and when and where   I don't care who said anything to
all right, I hope   I do hope that we're almost finished and done with
all this   this mess   yes   I suppose you might say that Mrs. Kahane
called because   as you say   misery loves company   afterward?
you mean after the phone call?   the testimony is that of Mr. Lewis
who told   somebody   that   I don't know who he told, it's not here
    he told somebody that   what?   I took it for granted that you
knew that Mr. Lewis was with the Henrys at their apartment   we've
been through all   yes, he lived with the Henrys and had been
freeloader is kind of a harsh   I told you that Mr. Henry was obligated
to him because he had arranged for the publication of   fine   I
thought for a minute that maybe you'd forgotten but you   God forbid
    you don't forget anything   only I tend to forget things, right?
right?   all right   Mr. Lewis said   it says   that Mrs. Henry did
tell Mrs. Kahane that she and Mr. Kahane had   they'd succumbed to
temptation and that she was truly   deeply sorry   she begged for
forgiveness   it all reads like a lot of baloney to   right   she got
down on her knees and begged her husband to   I don't know if that's
figurative or what it is   it was Mr. Lewis who said this   she got
down on her hands and knees and wept   oh boy   and wept bitterly
as she told Mr. Henry what had   Mr. Lewis says that she told her
husband that Mr. Kahane had   taken advantage of her in the
clothes closet   it says   right here   the clothes closet   that's a

new twist and it seems to me there's something wrong about it
because it's where   supposedly   Miss Lorpailleur and Mr. Harley
at the Christmas party   did something that was, you remember
said to be scandalous   I did! Jesus   I specifically recall telling you
that Miss Lorpailleur   fine   fine   as long as we don't start in
again on things we've already   and then what?   you mean at the
Henrys   oh   it goes on   Mr. Lewis goes on   to say   that Mr.
Henry wept and then began to shout and threw some papers around
and some other objects   an ash tray   a book or two   a lamp
and so on   and then he demanded that his wife do for him what
what she did for Mr. Kahane   what?   Mr. Lewis said that he retired
     left the room   so he didn't see whether or not Mrs. Henry   yes
there's one more thing   Mr. Lewis said that he heard Mr. Henry say
that he was damned if his wife was going to be a whore for Mr. Kahane
     too   I don't know who he   it might have been   yes   Mr.
Lewis that he   Mr. Henry was referring to   I've told you at least
ten times   Mr. Lewis had done Mr. Henry a favor with Mr. Blanche
Blanche Neige Press   in getting Mr. Henry's book   *The Orange*
Dress?   yes there's some evidence that Mr. Lewis interceded with
Mr. Blanche concerning *The Orange Dress* too   it could have been
could have   that Mrs. Henry was willing to   and Mr. Henry too
yes   willing to do favors   as you put it   for Mr. Lewis in return
for   who?   Cecil Tyrell?   he was   he was   let me see, he was
     he was somehow involved with *The Party*   the film project
that's all I know about   no   no mention of him at the party in any
way   any way at all   why do you mention   why do you bring him
up?

     You referred to some paper of agreement or contract that Lou
signed with or for Saul Blanche—what was that all about?

     I was waiting for you to bring that up   I'm surprised that you
didn't ask about it earlier   it's just the sort of thing that you'd find
really   yes I have all the answers   what a word   I have them all
here clipped together so that   here they are   if you'll bear with me
since this is complicated   what?   I can't understand it and I don't

want to   I don't get any pleasure out   I know you know   I just
thought I'd   all right   it appears that Mr. Henry signed a paper
or contract   whatever you want to call it   with Mr. Blanche   that
implicated him, Mr. Henry, in the business concerning the forgeries
of the prints   the forged prints that I told you about?   fine   I
wanted to make sure that you remem   anyway, Mr. Henry signed
this contract or whatever   that said   that made it clear   that he,
Mr. Henry   was instrumental in arranging for the purchase and
storage of paints and dyes and such   it says the prints themselves
here too   for the storage of these things in the basement of Mama
Gatto's and that he   Mr. Henry   was in on   that he was in on this
     scheme   concerning the forgeries with the rest of   once again?
     Mr. Blanche, Mr. Tete, Mr. Harley, and Mr. Gom   but   but it
appears that Mr. Henry was actually not and that he was duped
tricked   into signing this contract or what   contract, fine   signing it for Mr. Blanche by   Mr. Lewis   it's not especially clear but it
would seem that this contract   that it was then used by Mr. Blanche
as a kind of   used to   blackmail is the word   yes   I think the
word used in this report is   wait a minute   pressure   I'd accept
blackmail   yes   so it would seem   the reasons are   this is all
in the papers here we seem to have everything but the   the contract
itself is missing   I don't know if by design or acci   what?   I was
going to say that the reasons given are all   what's the word?
conjecture   conjectural   as a matter of fact they look so farfetched
that   of course I'll give them to   to the bitter end   after all, we
have so much proof of everything   built on sand   if I may say so
that we might as well build a little   I have no intention of wasting
your time   right   the reasons given   right   the rock-solid
brass-bound   unimpeachable reasons   right   Mr. Blanche was
angry and annoyed at Mr. Henry and at Mr. Lewis   and at Mrs. Lewis
too, I'd imagine   because   as you know   Blanche Neige Press
had published *The Orange Dress*   Mrs. Henry's   what was it?
it was   it was described as a   poetic novel about a doomed artist
a poet   a doomed poet   in any event it turned out that Mr. Henry

and Mr. Lewis who had done, you'll recall, a group of linoleum cuts
for the book it turned out that they knew that Mrs. Henry had not
actually it wasn't actually her work her book I mean that Mrs.
Henry had it would appear that *The Orange Dress* had been written
by someone else who had left it with Mrs. Henry and that she had
no there's no name mentioned but whoever it was committed
suicide I have no idea who it was why would I know who it
yes Mrs. Henry had discussed this manuscript with Mr. Henry and
they had perhaps with Mr. Lewis too, it doesn't make it clear precisely who they discussed it and what with one thing and another
and given the quality of the manuscript and that the author had been
a good friend well with this that and the other thing it was decided that it would be a good idea to get in touch with Mr. Blanche
to see if he would be interested in publishing *The Orange Dress* as
a novel by Mrs. Henry and so they what? it notes that this was
well, not notes there's a little note a sort of diagram here
that says Sheila and then there's an arrow that points to the name
April that would be Mrs. Detective and then another arrow
that points to the name Saul right Mrs. Henry got in touch
with Mrs. Detective because she Mrs. Detective was a neighbor of
you remember I'm glad that you remember something because I
I don't remember any I mean talk about convoluted certainly
I am going on ever onward well, to make a long story short
ha ha and ha Mr. Blanche published *The Orange Dress* as a as
being by Sheila Henry and it made a considerable stir in publishing
circles literary circles and was given raves in let me see
Bookwatchers PreViews and *Big Apple* and did as they say very
nicely for Blanche Neige it went into a third printing within the
year and there was some talk about a movie option so right
there is of course more to it it then happened somehow that Blanche
Neige the very next season published Mr. Henry's poems
Sheila Sleeping or *Lobster Lays* perhaps both, it's not clear
somehow? it looks as if there's some evidence hearsay evidence that Mr. Henry threatened he told Mr. Blanche that *The*

Orange Dress was by   someone other than Mrs. Henry   and that
if Mr. Blanche would publish Mr. Henry's poems then   exactly
you might say that   what people don't know won't hurt them or
something like   Mr. Lewis was   forced   I suppose is a fair
enough word   by Mr. Blanche to act as the agent   so to speak
in reference to the agreement   the contract   concerning the prints
      and so on and so forth   I suppose so, yes   the blackmailer was
blackmailed   so it seems   well he must have had something   as
you put it   on Mr. Lewis to recruit him as the   what did I call him?
      the agent   who got Mr. Henry to sign the   what?   I suppose
that Mr. Blanche might have had   I mean anything is possible
have had those photographs of Mrs. Lewis   I don't see what you're
driving   anything is possible but I don't know anything about
other photo   who?   Tania Crosse?   the way you suddenly   the
way these names pop up out of   you must think that I'm some kind
of a human computer or   Tania Crosse   all right   Miss Crosse
was   she was a photographer and she was   for a time   Mr.
Mr. Blanc's fiancée   and she also knew   right   she also knew
Mr. Blanche and assisted him at Blanche Neige   I remember that I
told you all this   definitely   and Mr. Blanc was also a photographer
      no   no   nowhere does it say that Mr. Blanc knew   or had even
met Mr. Blanche   of course it's possible!   that good old possible
if Miss Crosse was in Vermont with Mr. Blanche and Mr. Blanc was her
fiancé then   what?   once again and I hope that it's the last time
I hope that it's the   Mr. Blanc was a photographer   Mr. Blanc was
at one time Miss Crosse's fiancé   Mr. Blanc was involved with *The
Party*   the film   period
      What other people at Horace Rosette's?
      Other people, that's all   just other people   I mean a few
people stayed   apparently   at Mr. Rosette's after the party ended
to   I suppose   to talk and have a few laughs   maybe a nightcap
just other people outside of Mr. Pungoe and Mr. Tete   so far as our
I like that our   so far as our   I'm sorry, and Mr. Hicks, of course
the world-famous Inspector of Buildings, known in song and   all

right   so far as our information goes   outside of Mr. Pungoe and
Mr.   I'm only trying to be as precise as   there were Mr. Moses, Mr.
Buckie-Moeller, Mr. Towne, Mrs. Lewis, and   either   Miss Lorpailleur or Sister Rose Zeppole   or maybe both of them   I don't
know   I mean I don't know!   look for yourself   see?   it says
Lorpailleur and under that Sister Rose and then there's a   what do
they call this?   I don't know   a little sort of   parenthesis
anyway, this little   bracket   that's it   bracket   and then a question mark   that would seem to mean that it could be either one or
fine, you agree   will wonders never   what were they what?   up
to?   I know what this junk tells me   and it doesn't tell me much
if you ask me they were hanging around to have a nightcap and sort
of wind down after the   wind down, wind down   God   you know
what I mean   you'd think that we don't speak the same language or
something like   I mean   to be specific   relax a little the way
people will tend to   I don't have any idea what they talked about
I don't have any idea what they did   what?   no   I don't have any
idea why the people who stayed stayed   oh fine   fine   that's a
little nasty   I think maybe this is getting on your nerves as much as
all right, not   I repeat   not   to answer in kind, I do know what
my name is but what I know about this after-party   gathering   is
exactly what I have here and it is very   sketchy   incomplete   of
course   as a matter of fact you can have it framed if you like   in
precious metals   I'll read it   I said I'd   I thought that we were
almost finished with this   I don't even know what to call what we're
doing   I   will   read   it   in all its blinding clarity   Page
Moses slash Chico Zeek colon Moses Z's name when doing comms
comms   that's what it says   c o m m s   I don't know   and if
you're going to ask me what this   shorthand   means I really don't
think that we ought to even bother about this because   it's all that
way   little stupid scratches and abbreviations and   all right
Page Moses slash Chico Zeek colon Moses Z's name when doing
comms Z slash belt slash Pungoe all he likes for more film dollar sign
Bunny too w Pungoe and Z via Ted's suggest also Pungoe dollar sign

here in re slash So West Devel Co Jackson in Annie's uniform and she as mother sup Hicks will prob sign o.k. anything Rosette bustles as host slash ess and Barn voyeur and shifts Annie slash tux Jack slash wimple and ling dollar sign to Z and Ted and Bunny to b slash r w Annie var phone calls April slash Sheila slash Lo K somebody lost und question mark refresh for all scene of LA work in prog question mark

and then it's signed Sylvie   that is   as they say   that   Annie?

I suppose Annie Flammard, I don't know of any other Annie   no she's not named as being there   not named as being anywhere for that matter   I told you   Miss Lorpailleur and Sister Rose   or Sister Rose   with the little bracket next to their   who?   it would seem that Sylvie is Miss Lacruseille   Sylvie Lacruseille   who is also not named   leads me to believe?   leads me to believe nothing since I can't make heads or tails out of who is who or who was who or who is liable to be who   or when   or why   I told you   a few laughs   a nightcap maybe   a kind of relax   I didn't tell you what?

oh   I see   I didn't really notice that   it says   *The Party* like a   heading, a title   like the title we've talked   that's all   there's nothing about anybody discussing or doing anything insofar as making a   Duke who?   oh, Duke Washington   yes, he was at the party   at least he's on the list but I don't have any idea who he is what do you mean   real?   I have no idea   as a matter of fact as far as I'm concerned they're all just names   as far as any of them being real or   *Hellions in Hosiery*?   oh God, are we going back to

no I don't care what I do or don't do   it's immaterial to me but I thought that we were going to wind this whole thing   I've got it I've got it here   *Hellions in Hosiery*   the stars   what a laugh that is   stars   the stars were Annie Flammard and Baylor Freeq you'll forgive me if I mention   if I whisper   if I dare to suggest that we've been over this so many   what do you mean what else?   oh Annie Flammard played a schoolteacher named   Marcella Butler and Baylor Freeq was a repairman   this was certainly a really profound movie   named   well   Duke Washington   I didn't say so before because you didn't ask   it must be obvious to you that the

more information I give you the more you confuse and involve and
mix up the   it's in a   you'll pardon the expression   press kit
a few mimeographed sheets is more like it   this was not exactly
a mammoth production   an extravaganza   Marcella Butler?   I
don't recall mentioning that name at all   I say I don't recall it   I
don't know why Duke Washington is on the party guest list   I thought
we were through with the damn party   maybe it was some kind of a
mistake   maybe it had something to do with *The Party*   the film
project   or whatever it was   maybe it was   I don't know   you
know I'm about   I'm really fed up   Miss Butler?   fine!   if you
say that I said that she was on the other   then that's fine   that's
absolutely fine   Miss Butler was a world-renowned molecular biologist   a Nobel laureate   and a distinguished professor   also a
loving wife a devoted mother and a pillar of the community who had
round heels   yes   it is my little joke   can we wrap this up?
just get it over and done with?   Miss Butler and Mr. Washington were
     apparently   not real   they were characters   names   that's
two down and the rest to   I mean if we play our cards right maybe
we can turn the whole bunch of them into just   make all of them
unreal   then maybe we can wrap the whole   I don't get any pleasure out of all   Biggs Richard?   I never heard of him   no   never
     a blank   fine   I told you   if you say so then it's fine with me
yes   cooperate?   of course   it's just that the more we find out
about these char   I was going to say characters   these people
the more we realize that we don't know any   hardly anything about
them, they just get more and more un   sure, we can talk about
anybody you like   Miss Tate?   right   here   on the party list
I mean the people who attended the   right   there's nothing about
any activity of hers at the party   and only one other thing   she was
apparently a neighbor of Mr. Detective's at one time   I have two old
leases with her name and Mr. Detective's   you can see for   you
can see   the same address   same place   Mr. Detective in Cottage
33 and Miss Tate in Cottage   I can't make it out   but there doesn't
seem to be anything   no, it's as you can see   Tate with an a not an

e   in *Isolate Flecks*?   I don't know that book but I'm sure I mentioned something   no I didn't know that Buffie Tate is a character in
    I agree that Grey Crimson sounds like a nom de   nom   a pen
name   no   nowhere   not a mention
        Why did Leo Kaufman leave Rosette's with Anne instead of El-
len?
        There are conflicting accounts here if you'll bear with me
for a moment   as if you haven't been or is it that I'm bearing with
yes   here are a number of accounts   again   oh Christ   again
one from Miss Schmidt who seems to have been everywhere   she
says that   she   wait a minute   this is all post-party material
it says   she says   that Mr. Kaufman was in a rear booth in some
bar with Mrs. Kaufman   Anne Kaufman   and he was crying   he
was crying and telling her   Mrs. Kaufman   his ex   all right, I
want to be sure you know exactly   telling her that he was sorry
that he should never have allowed   Duke   Duke?   he should
never have allowed Duke to move in with them when they were so
happy together   it says   Duke   I can only guess that he means
Mr. Washington so it looks like this information   press kit   about
Hellions in Hosiery is so much hog   what?   it could have been Mr.
Freeq but why would Miss Schmidt call   well I know, Miss Schmidt
I know what I said!   but it's possible she could write   don't you
think so?   you don't have to be able to talk to know how to   I don't
know how she could have heard   right   I never thought of that
I don't know how   all right   he was crying and saying that he had
been a fool to let Duke whoever move in with them   he didn't care
what this Duke had on him   he shouldn't have let him do it because
he knew   the account goes on   he knew that she   his ex-wife
Anne Kaufman   he knew that she'd fall for his line and that   things
    would happen   and then his ex-wife said that she didn't   she
wouldn't have done anything   wouldn't have been such a   I can't
make this out   wouldn't have been such a something   if   he
Mr. Kaufman   hadn't insisted on it being a nightly thing and did he
Mr. Kaufman   think that she was happy doing all those things

with him   watching?   and sometimes other people too?   then
Mr. Kaufman cried some more and   sat next to her in the booth and
said that if Mr. Washington hadn't had the snapshots would she have
wait a minute   I have to find the rest   would she have   would
she have   that's all I have here   there must be something miss
oh here it is   would she have   wait a minute   there must be
I think a sheet is missing because this starts   I'll read it   but Anne
said that it was better just to take off with Duke than put up with this
degradation so that he could get some flunky job with that bastard
Whitestone   what?   he?   I guess   Mr. Kaufman but   it's not
clear   then Mr. Kaufman started to cry harder and they left the bar
and Mrs. Kaufman   Anne Kaufman   took him to her apartment in
     wait a minute   in a taxi   don't ask me!   I don't know what any
of this means   here's another account by   Mademoiselle Aubois
very brief   drunk as usual Leo stumbled out with the whore   that's
one and here's another   the whore?   well this is supposed to be
about Mr. Kaufman and his first wife   and his second   present
wife   so it might be that the whore is Mrs. Anne   I'm telling you
that's all it says   and then one more by Miss Ostrom   that says that
     Mr. Kaufman was very drunk as was Mrs. Kaufman   Anne Kauf-
man   and that the present Mrs. Kaufman   Ellen Kaufman
what?   I do like to be as you say formal   I think it's better to stay
as objective as poss   fine   Mr. Kaufman and his first wife were
drunk and his present wife   as far as Miss Ostrom knew   his present wife surprised them making love   the account says out   making out   in Mr. Rosette's study for   an audience   then?   how
should I know?   oh, Miss Ostrom's   then, Miss Ostrom says   that
that would probably finish Mr. Kaufman as far as sponging off his wife
     I would guess, yes, his present wife   Ellen Kaufman   I suppose
     when I say present I don't mean present present   now   you
know what I mean   fine   those are the accounts   if you'll pardon
the   like all of these   accounts and depositions   testimony
eyewitness this and that   and the notes and   the photographs
none of this seems to jell no matter   none of it seems to paint a

Mr. Kaufman?   he was   he was   hm   he had been a poet
had a small reputation as a poet when he married for the first time
and then he   wrote reviews and gave readings and   let's see
here's a contract   two contracts   to teach somewhere   some
writing workshop   then   then   he did some free-lance work for
    Crescent and Chattaway, some   publishers   I told you they were
publishers   I don't know why I bother to keep going through all this
junk when you forget   maybe you don't forget   all right   but it
certainly seems as if   all right   all right!   Crescent and Chattaway when Mr. Whitestone was there   but he   it was only free-
lance   he   Mr. Kaufman   never got on the payroll   then
here's a photostat of a final divorce decree   then it looks like   it's
a wedding invitation   Mr. and Mrs. Jack Marowitz and so forth and
so on   it just warms your heart   a real all-American story
everything in such nice order   I am getting crazy   then   then
Jesus!   there's just so much crap here   can I cut it short?   can I
just sort of   all right   the essentials   thank you   Mr. Kaufman
started drinking   heavy drinking   and Mr. Marowitz supported
no   Mrs. Marow   I mean Mrs. Kaufman   Ellen Kaufman   had
an allowance from her father and she supported her husband because
she thought that he was a great artist and decided to   she supported
him because she thought that he was a great poet   that's what it says
    a great poet   but he just kept   he was a hopeless drunk   so
Mrs. Kaufman would cut him off   his allowance   what?   there's
a copy of a page here from a   diary?   no   an account book I guess
    not a diary   it could be I guess   yes   but this page is a page of
accounts   I fail to understand why you blow the smallest things out
of all   who cares whether it could be a diary or an account book or
a notebook or an address   right   it says   it shows   God forbid
that I should say says   it shows that Mrs. Kaufman gave Mr. Kaufman
    let's see   twelve and two-fifty and ten and   let's see   she gave
him thirty dollars a week?   I guess a week   but she would sometimes increase   according to a deposition   another deposition
by Miss Lorpailleur who at the time   it says that she was a maid at

the Marowitz house   but I seem to recall that she wasn't?   or it
was said   sworn   that she wasn't a real maid?   is that right?
is that the fact?   or am I   fine   Miss Lorpailleur   the trustwor-
thy Miss Lorpailleur said that Mrs. Kaufman told her father that she
would cut Mr. Kaufman off   so he wouldn't drink I suppose   and
no Miss Lorpailleur doesn't say that   I say that   I have a right I
think to an occasional opinion   what else?   that's about all
what?   that's all   what?   this? oh, I didn't see it   on the back of
the wedding announce   of course I'll read it   we aim to please
ask and you shall receive   I know you're tired   at the top of the
card   typed   it says   Leo's Last Poem   then underneath   in
a very clear handwriting by the way   it doesn't look at all like what
you'd expect Mr. Kaufman's   it says   first line   I love   second
line   your can   third line   did tits   I'm not making it up
look for your   see?   I love   your can   did tits   I don't know
much about poetry but if this is poetry   no wonder he became a
drunk   Ellen Kaufman?   there's absolutely nothing here but I
don't think that she would have any   trouble, as you put it   getting
home from Mr. Rosette's   why? Mr. Gom   you remember that Mr.
Marowitz had the money that   for Christ sake he probably would
have been happy to carry her   piggyback   I don't know how Lincstone was doing   but a bird in the hand

    What's that about Lucy Taylor at Lou and Sheila's?

    I mentioned this already when I told you about the phone call
from Mrs. Kahane to Mrs. Henry   what did I tell you?   this is really
too much for   I told you that Mr. Henry and Mrs. Henry and Mr. Lewis
had left the party   and etcetera   and that Miss Taylor had left with
them   because she'd been on the outs with Miss Jefferson   you
recall Miss Jefferson?   Lorzu?   do you recall Miss   right   you
ask   I answer   anyway   Miss Taylor and Miss Jefferson had had
  let me see   they'd had a business disagreement over some bill
wait a   here's the bill   made out to Harlan Pungoe   and according to a letter written by Miss Taylor Mr. Pungoe had never paid the
in the amount of twelve hundred and sixty-seven dollars and forty-

nine cents   and Mr. Pungoe had never   for lingerie   lingerie and
undergarments   and some specialty items   lingerie, lingerie
of course I can give you a general   camisoles, teddies, panties, bras,
corsets, garter belts, a   bustier?   whatever that may be   nylon
hosiery   the usual   the other items are   a maid's uniform   a
nurse's uniform   a habit   it says   I guess a nun's habit   yes,
well   here is   according to a preliminary statement   Miss Taylor
wanted Mr. Pungoe to pay this bill and Miss Jefferson wanted to write
it off   I don't know   yes   that was the cause of the disagreement
according to   yes   Miss Jefferson went her way and Miss Taylor
I told you this   Miss Taylor went with the Henrys and Mr. Lewis to
the Henrys' apartment   what makes me think I did?   because I
know I did!   certainly I can   surely I can   back into the boxes
back to the trusty files where everything true and good is recorded for
     I am annoyed   Miss Taylor was   had been   an art student
a water colorist of   it says   limited talents   this appraisal
appraisal?   whatever   it says   from a teacher   it says   possible talent for undemanding communal   no   commercial art
then   just a second   then she met Mr. Lewis and they had lived
together for a   well, he   Mr. Lewis   had lived with Miss Taylor
it was her apartment   what?   well   I don't know if living off other
people was   as you say   his chief talent   she also lived with a
painter or a sculptor   I don't know his name   he worked with
chicken wire and rags?   that's what it says   maybe after   maybe
before   these documents   these scraps of paper I should say
don't have any dates on   I don't know if she was   back together
with Mr. Lewis   all it says is that she accompanied him to the Henrys'
apartment   after the party at Mr. Rosette's had broken   Mr. Lewis
was driving and Miss Taylor sat next to him and the Henrys were in
the back   what?   according to   it says that Mr. Lewis had his
hand on Miss Taylor's thigh   it doesn't say whether his hand was
under   this is Mrs. Henry's statement   I don't know what they were
doing in the back   looking up at the mysterious stars   contem-
plating the swift passage of time   reciting deathless poetry to   of

course it says   Mrs. Henry says   that it was indeed Miss Taylor
why wouldn't it be Miss   wearing?   now how am I   yes, now that
you mention it I   this is a   it looks like a clipping   Miss Taylor
modeled, and quite beautifully   a sleeveless shift of   off-white raw
silk in the new shorter length designed to reveal the patterned stockings that promise to be the season's hottest item   no it's not   necessarily   necessarily strange   as you put it   that Miss Taylor
might have been wearing the same   on the other hand   what leads
you to believe that Miss Taylor was wearing this clothing   on this
particular night?   I mean   why would you think that Miss Taylor
would wear something that she apparently model   I said that Mrs.
Henry stated that it was Miss Taylor that accomp   what?   they had
a drink   and then the phone call from Mrs. Kahane   and then Mr.
Henry   do we have to go through   and then the business with Mr.
Henry and Mrs. Henry begging him to   Mr. Lewis had gone into another room   that's what it   as I recall   said   this account?
this account is by   it's anonymous   I don't know   maybe somebody was looking in the window   how should I know who knew what
     maybe it's a lie   maybe all of this is a lie   I'm doing my   I went
to a lot of trouble to   this account says that   Mr. Lewis went into
wait a minute   I have to find the other   that Mr. Lewis went into
the bathroom with Miss Taylor   when Mr. and Mrs. Henry began
their private   discussion   and that Mrs. Henry   stumbled on
them when she went to use the bathroom   she stumbled on them at
precisely the moment at which Mr. Lewis was about to   I can't read
it   Miss Taylor   and that she was shocked at Miss Taylor's abandon
     abandoned position   that's it in its entire   yes there is   not a
photograph but   I guess it's a copy of   a xerox copy of   yes   it
looks like a shift   no I can't see the woman's face   I mean I can see
it but   it's blurred because the copy   like who?   Mrs. Lewis?
I wouldn't say that   besides we have evidence   evidence is some
mouthful   we have evidence that Mrs. Lewis stayed at Mr. Rosette's
so that   how should I know when it was taken   or copied?   it's
with this stuff   this crap   this   about what happened   maybe

at the Henrys' apartment   an effort to what?   it was   believe me
    hard enough to get it all together   what I could of it   without
verifying any   what?   Mr. Lewis is referred to as   let me check
he's referred to as L in this statement   I suppose it's possible that L
could stand for Lou   why not?   it's also possible that Mrs. Henry
could have been with Mr. Lewis in the living room   you know
there's nothing   absolutely nothing   nothing that I've told you that
hasn't been made into   made into some kind of a   what's that thing
you do with a strip of paper where you twist it and then   you put the
ends together?   so that you can't tell where   you can't tell one side
from another?   what do they call that?   that's how you twist things
    everything I say   you twist

        What did Whitestone, Gom, and Miss Ostrom talk about in the
bar to which they went afterward?

        Oh God   I have a   what do they   a dossier an inch thick
on   I don't know   maybe a waiter   or bartender   I really don't
know   all right   not quite an inch   but if you want me   really
to really read this then we'll be here for a   what?   oh the sheets
stapled together   all right   that's better   I'll start   yes, at the
beginning   beginning is a hell of a word to use don't you think?   I
mean   beginning!   why don't we start going back into their childhood so that we can see what happened to them   like they do in those
big fat novels   those what do they call them?   good reads   then
we can understand everything   you know   like somebody saw his
mother putting a present under the Christmas tree   not Santa
his mother so that the kid knows that there's no Santa   some pathetic
little thing   a windup toy or something   a little soldier   or a tin
yes   sorry   Mr. Whitestone said that it was a hell of a   what?
I don't have to read   general statements?   fine   the core is what
you'll get   the really deep and important   the gold!   Mr. Whitestone said that   he thought that maybe they should seriously con-
sider giving Miss Lorpailleur a role   settle things peaceably with
it doesn't say what   *The Party* I guess   the film business   settle
things   and Mr. Gom thought that was a good idea   something

here   a rather garbled note   about how he   or they   agreed
that she   Miss Lorpailleur   had no   no something   to make
trouble over the plagiarism thing   and there's the name Léonie Aubois in a little box   a box drawn around it   and then   let me see,
a new page   she mentioned that Miss Lorpailleur had told her that
I would guess Miss Ostrom?   she   it only says she   that Miss
Lorpailleur had told her that Miss Lacruseille was a very powerful
figure   a friend   and   chair?   what this is I   oh   she chaired
some international authors' organization that looked into these situations in order to pro   that's what I thought too   that she was
so to speak   Miss Lacruseille   that Miss Lacruseille wasn't real
just a name   why did I tell   for Christ sake?   I told you what these
    dossiers   say   I can't help it if they don't say what you want them
to say   maybe if you asked different questions we'd get to the bottom
of   whatever it is   whatever it is you're trying to find out   what?
    see?   you're doing this again   hopping around from this to that
in no order at   all right!   material on Miss Ostrom material on
Miss Ostrom material on Miss Ostrom material on   yes   first of all
    no mention here of her activities with Miss Lorpailleur at Mr. Ro-
sette's   that's number one   a remark by Mr. Gom to the effect that
she   that he   Mr. Gom   thought that she   Miss Ostrom   had
the most beautiful legs that he'd ever seen and that he'd really like
I suppose so   yes   that he'd seen plenty of them at the party
and then   number   number three   Mr. Whitestone suggested
that Miss Ostrom do her best to please her while they figured out what
to do about her threat   a veiled threat?   I suppose so   concerning
the   concerning Miss Lacruseille and so forth and so on   no
please her is not spelled out   yes, right   that's all on Miss Ostrom
three little   what? what would who really like?   Mr. Gom?   I
don't know what you   oh yes   I'm sorry   you   as usual
interrupted me   you know if we could just follow one line of   Mr.
Gom said that he'd really like to see the rest of them   legs   Miss
Ostrom's legs!   God   that's it   one no mention of party scene two
legs three please Miss Lorpailleur and that's that for   trusty faithful

hardworking and bright Miss Os   yes yes yes   to the stars!   Mr.
Whitestone and Mr. Gom were most concerned though that Miss Lorpailleur   because she was Mr. Marowitz's maid   there are little
quote marks around that word and then   in a   in parentheses
the word laughter   because she was   she definitely   there was
a definite possibility that she knew a lot about the   stock deal   and
this was a problem that they couldn't   it says stock deal   no   I've
never heard of anything like it   I mean   you know   come across
anything that   anyway they couldn't afford such a problem because

if Mr. Marowitz thought that he'd be implemented   implicated
he'd drop the gallery   pull out his money   then a note in the mar-
gin   here   see?   says   Tete pressure certain   and then
Mr. Whitestone notes   if Mr. Marowitz for whatever reason blacks
out?   oh   backs   backs out   there goes Lincstone   Mr. Gom
added here that if he   himself   were involved in any public
publicity concerning the stocks   that too would mean the end of
Lincstone   they might as well fold and take a   take a something
it's illegible   then one of the men   it doesn't say which   one of
them said they might as well give the fucking bitch a part in the thing

or else it might all go down the drain   Miss Ostrom?   I guess
she was just listening   there's nothing   I told you   nothing other
than the three   and   fine   and the other man agreed and said
maybe they could give Miss Lorpailleur a part and also make an
agreement?   yes   an agreement with Miss Aubois on credits
whatever that means   now   there's a page or two here about possible screenplays   people to write   yes   I'll read the watermark
if you want   I am tired, yes   it's a goddam list   it says   Dick D,
Whytte-Blorenge, Lorna, Léonie A   then   here's some more on
what seems to be   yes   the last page thank Jesus   Mr. Whitestone
says   or   yes   Mr. Whitestone says that there is still a problem
with Mr. Pungoe whom they   Mr. Pungoe was more or less promised
that Annie Flammard would be very seriously considered for the
for a role   because she'd been so good   had   it says   made a
splash with hip people   in *Hellions in Hosiery* and Mr. Gom added

don't forget *Silk Thighs* and *Sisters in Satin*   then they talked about
   grosses and earnings   what?   no figures are included   then
let me see   then Mr. Whitestone says that that   would be a problem
   the Annie Flammard thing   and Mr. Gom says that Mr. Pungoe
admired her a great deal and thought she had a lot of talent   and
talent is   it's got quote marks around it   like the word before that
I   right   Mr. Whitestone says that that   plus the fact   that?
I suppose that refers to the fact that Mr. Pungoe wanted Miss Flammard to have a role in *The Party*   anyway   he says that that plus
the fact that Mr. Pungoe and Mr. Tete were also involved in business
together could mean that they couldn't even defend on   depend on
Mr. Pungoe's share of the backing   then someone says   whoever
says that Mr. Pungoe might not be a problem after all because Mr.
Lewis seemed   persuaded?   persuaded that it would be wise to
ask his wife   who else?   of course   to ask her to entertain Mr.
Pungoe and that she might be doing that right now   it says   as we
speak   entertain?   that's all it says   it doesn't say how or where
I don't know   why would I have an opinion about Mrs. Lewis?   no
   there's nothing more   just that they left   they stiffed the waiter
       Well, what was the substance of April and Dick's conversation?
       Well   the substance   why don't I give you   it would be
easier to give you the important   so to speak   the important information   I have a transcript from the tape here and   no   I won't
withhold any pertinent data   just drop the hums and the ohs and the
ahs the   well   personal relations because it appears that about
about halfway through their talk they had an   interlude   they
it appears that they made love and they say   a lot of   well   intimate things   they speak rather intimately to   they say sexual
things   they ask each other to   do things   I don't think it's important   as a matter of fact anybody who'd want to know this sort of
thing is   it's not something that anybody would want to know   it's
bad enough that we're   yes I will   they were talking over the party
and   the real party they were just at   and Mr. Detective said
that was some scene with good old Bart and Sheila in the bathroom

what a surprise to me and I guess everyone because I thought that it was Guy who was getting into Sheila's pants   and Mrs. Detective said that   she said   you're really terrible besides it wasn't the bathroom scene that was so bad it was later when Horace and I walked in on them in Horace's bedroom and Sheila was at it really hot and heavy

and Mr. Detective said   if I didn't know that Horace mine host was as queer as a three-dollar bill I'd be a little annoyed with you going into his bedroom like that   what by the way did you want to do there?

and Mrs. Detective said   I wanted to talk to him or rather he wanted to talk to you but you were as usual making a fool of yourself with Rose so he decided to talk to me   it was about I think because we never did talk at any length because of the wild scene but I think it was about asking you to contribute something to a new anthology of his something about cities a collection of pieces on cities?   and Mr. Detective   Horace can go fuck himself with his dollar fifty a page I'm sick of him with his cheap shit and his poor mouth   but what exactly was Sheila   what were Sheila and Bart up to?   and Mrs. Detective   well Sheila was on her hands and knees with half her clothes off and Bart was behind her giving it to her in her backside but the worst part is that and I think we ought to keep this really quiet the worst part is that that poor sick bastard Lou was sitting in a chair watching them and jerking himself off and groaning   my God they were all so stoned out of their minds that they didn't even see us or hear us   and Mr. Detective   Jesus Christ!   and Mrs. Detective I was so embarrassed that I couldn't even look at any of them later and Mr. Detective   you've gotten pretty modest in your old age haven't you?   and Mrs. Detective   exactly what does that mean? you're going to bring up those goddam pictures again after all these years?   and Mr. Detective   no I'm sorry but when I think about how that son of a bitch rube Pungoe used those pictures to get us to persuade persuade is some word for it persuade those poor ignorant bastards to sign away that acreage that son of a bitch!   and Mrs. Detective   well it's all water under the bridge and the best thing is to forget all about it don't you think so?   and Mr. Detective   I suppose you're right but when I think of that bastard leering at those pictures and my God!   that good wonderful true blue old pal from school days Tania conning you with how the pictures would get us back together again Jesus!   I could just   and I still can't figure out why you didn't think something was funny when she laid out all that for Christ sake a thousand dollars' worth of fancy underwear and those costumes I mean I still can't figure out why you didn't realize that something was fishy   and Mrs. Detective   I thought we weren't going to bring this up?   and Mr. Detective   I'm sorry   then there's this   as I said   interlude   Mr. and Mrs. Detective make love   what?   no not as I recall   no mention earlier at all of Mr. Henry in   well you have it all down there   don't you?   no there's no mention of Mrs. Detective writing to him   I told you I wouldn't leave   of course   Mr. Detective said   you know the whole thing reminds me of the time we went to that party that dinner party when Roberte Flambeaux got caught in the clothes closet with some dirty old lecher by Lorna do you remember that?   and Mrs. Detective   oh God yes and Roberte said God she was drunk Roberte said that she was just doing what Lorna only wrote about remember?

and Mr. Detective   the old bastard said he thought she was only a maid hired for the night for the party I'll never forget Roberte's fiancé's face what was his name?   and Mrs. Detective   I don't remember but he'd just about gotten over Lorna's book when that had to happen I wonder what ever happened to Roberte?   and Mr. Detective   I heard that she was working as a buyer for ZuZu and what's her name but I can't see how a little shop like that can afford a buyer and Mrs. Detective   I don't even know how they can afford the rent at that location let alone a buyer   and Mr. Detective   speaking of money I heard a rumor from Karen that Whitestone might ask me to do a treatment for *The Party*, which would be great if it's true and also if I knew what a fucking treatment is and how to write one   and Mrs. Detective   that seems strange to me when they can get Craig Garf probably I wonder where Karen got that idea?   and Mr. Detective I was thinking about it myself and all I could figure is that the author of the novel that French writer I don't remember her name or the name of the book for that matter thinks that maybe it's a way of getting me in between her and Annette because you know that big scene at the party about who really wrote the book or whatever the hell they were screaming about and she figures that I'm a good friend of Annette's wherever she got that idea   and Mrs. Detective   well let's not count our chickens God I'd like to be a fly on the wall when Sheila or I should say when Lou starts crying tonight about what a whore she is in front of Guy and probably asking Guy's advice my God!   and Mr. Detective   that's their problem why don't we go to sleep?   and Mrs. Detective   uh-huh   and that's the end of the transcript Mademoiselle Aubois?   I don't know why she'd think they were good friends   except   well   except that if Miss Lorpailleur and Sister Rose Zeppole were the same woman   we had some testimony? or some kind of   possibility or something? if you'll recall   something about it anyway   if Mademoiselle Aubois knew   or thought that Miss Lorpailleur and Sister Rose were the same person   then she might think that because   she might know that Mr. Detective and Sister Rose   that is maybe Miss Lorpailleur   knew each other because of what somebody   or some paper or witness or something had said   about Sister Rose and Mr. Detective when he and Mrs. Detective were separated   what?   I can't remember exactly but it was something about Sister Rose being of some help to him   you might remember the ref   S I what?   S I S?   no   no   I can't recall that at all   I said I can't!   I'd really like   very much like to wrap this up now   do you think that we

And to whom was Léonie Aubois saying all this?

Well   I was about to tell you   that's the trouble with this sh this data here in this blue folder   it not only doesn't make clear who was involved   it mentions a number of names but there's no absolute   no specific   well Mademoiselle Aubois of course   then maybe Mr. and Mrs. Harley and Mr. Freeq   or   Mr. Harley and Miss Schmidt   or Miss Schmidt and Mrs. Harley   or maybe all of them what was I   oh yes   it not only doesn't make clear who exactly was

involved   but it doesn't indicate who said what   only just what was
said   fine   sure   God knows, it can't be any more impossible
than the rest of   yes I will!   somebody said   I'll just say   it was
said   all right?   it was said that Miss Lorpailleur's book was not a
book at all and that Mademoiselle Aubois took the junk   all the
scraps and unfinished scenes   the anecdotes and such   and made
a real   a beautiful work of art   and that Miss Lorpailleur's book
anyway   outside of it being just a kind of notebook   a kind of journal   wasn't even fiction   wasn't shared   shaped   wasn't
shaped at all but was based on things she did when she was working
as a maid   a so-called maid   for some neurotic couple because
she'd do anything for a dollar   and she kept a kind of diary there
that's all *Mouth of Steel* was   just a title on a jumble of diary entries
     a diary of this couple's very strange pastimes   this couple would
write little plays   weird and perverse plays and have friends over to
act them out it must have been like   La Coste?   yes   it says La
Coste   whatever that means   and   and   right   and Miss
Lorpailleur thought she could cash in on this with some self-styled
fearless publisher   lucky for that   no   lucky for the world that
Mr. Harley saw the possibilities and that the mass   the mess   the
mess found its way to Mademoiselle Aubois   and all this pretentious
planted   these pretentious planted rumors that Miss Lorpailleur is
a known writer who works under the name of Sylvie Lacruseille
what an incredible nerve   it's well known that Miss Lorpailleur's
real name is Sylvie Lacruseille and that Annette Lorpailleur   strictly
confidentially but it wouldn't hurt if everyone somehow found out
Annette Lorpailleur   according to someone who should know
Annie Flammard   Annette Lorpailleur is a name that she got out of
some novel   so you see the brazen   the unbelievable nerve of the
woman   and to make it worse   to threaten Mademoiselle Aubois
with a suit   it is too vulgar   as if *La Soirée intime* owes really
anything   anything at all to that almost illiterate pile of scrawls
to treat Mademoiselle Aubois as if she were no better than Mrs. Henry
     and what about Mrs. Henry?   well   one thought by now that

everybody   it's almost public knowledge   in any event   an open
secret   Mrs. Henry simply put her name on somebody else's com-
pleted manuscript   *The Orange Dress*   some poor man who took
those disgusting Henrys into his confidence   can't recall his name
something like Cedric   or Charles something   Cedric Try   Cecil
Tyrell!   of course   for Miss Lorpailleur to suggest that what   or
even to imply that what Mademoiselle Aubois did is in any remote way
the same as what Mrs. Henry   well   he committed suicide is what
people say   he'd given the manuscript to his dear oh very dear
friends the Henrys   and she lost no time in having it retyped   was
that a Crescent and Chattaway book?   it seems as if it should have
been what with Mr. Whitestone with his eye for the daring and
adventurous?   adventurous new writer if you'll pardon the expression   good old Mr. Whitestone   loved   absolutely loved daring
and exciting fiction   fiction that employed the greatest daring and
freedom and experimentation but the kind of judicious experimentation that doesn't look with contempt on the reader of good will the
common reader   the sort of fiction that is extremely daring and experimental and free but that has a strong moral purpose and a mes-
sage of hope and humanity for all humankind and so on and so forth
what good old Mr. Whitestone would say   oh yes   of course it
should have been but even Mr. Whitestone smelled a rat   apparently
     how could Sheila Henry have written a book like *The Orange Dress*
after those years and years   and years   of the most idiotic little
poems   let's not forget her little experimental   oh God   para-
graphs full of her utterly pedest   pedest   oh   pedestrian and
vulgar erotic fantasies   she called them bursts of energy didn't she?
     oh Jesus   she should have said busts   so then if it wasn't Mr.
Whitestone who   oh of course   Blanche Neige   what else?
and what is so amusing   if it doesn't make you sick   what is so
amusing is that Mr. Henry then published some dull collection of
poems   Blanche Neige again   the Henrys were becoming a cottage industry   and Saul Blanche also published that dreary *Black-*
jack by Mr. Detective   or his wife?   who knows?   isn't that the
one about the stealing?   that's the book about someone   yes

someone stealing somebody else's book and becoming famous   and
the fame   oh it's too ghastly   a Connecticut soap opera   it's too
ridiculous   the fame ruins him   God it's too fucking precious for
you don't know the book? oh God it's literally   quite literally beyond

that scene in front of the fire when the hero rhapsodies   rhapsod-
izes   on his first year of marriage and his wife's plaid skirt   from
Peck and Peck   sweet bleeding and suffering Jesus   it turns out
that he wants her to leave the skirt on while he screws her   right
but he's ashamed to ask because of what he knows   oh brother
what he knows turns out to be that she is innocence   don't forget
the capital I   she is innocence and he is corruption   perversity
one can't even be that hilarious intentionally   well all right   but
it's hard not to be hilarious writing about the suburbs   what a book
it must have been very weird for Mrs. Henry though   given   right

but to get back to Miss Lorpailleur   Mademoiselle Aubois thought
it best to make some kind of peace with her   after all, Lincstone was
about to start looking for a screenwriter and legal difficulties and so
on would simply delay things   Miss Lorpailleur might accept a
credit and she could even perhaps   collaborate   not really   but
act as a consultant   give her some kind of a title   money   money
of course would have to be offered and be right   that's all she really
cares about   and perhaps a dinner party   some kind of a party to
make her feel   right   but the guest list will not   not   include
Mrs. Henry   not after that awkward scene that night at   where
was it?   oh yes   at Mr. Rosette's publication party when she was
locked in the bathroom with   well   some say it was with Mrs.
Kaufman   God knows which one   and others say it was Mr. Kahane

who has   it's well known   no taste at all   if you look at his
work over the past few years   anyone can see that he's lost   maybe
washed   and that's it   it breaks off right there   no questions?
you're actually not going to ask any questions?   this has got to be
some kind of a

Why is it that so much of what you've told me also happens,
more or less, in *Isolate Flecks*?

That's really   really too much   for the last   I hope I dearly hope   for the last time I   right here   see?   I haven't told you anything that's a n y t h i n g   this   these all these papers   this testimony and data and reports   eyewitness reports anonymous reports   these transcripts and depositions   and   God!   diaries this crap   this shit   you ask and I answer and always   almost always   before I can finish you ask some more and some more and some more   and I find   or try to find   something that will do that will answer   if you think that what all this   all this is   is just some   from some fucking novel   why don't you read the novel and get all the answers right there?   read it and get everything   get all of it   and if the names are different in the novel just put the right ones in   substitute the right ones   they don't matter anyway   all these people might as well be   all these people are just names anyway   as far as I'm concerned   don't ask me   ask the novel what?   I have   as far as I'm concerned I have answered the question   I've answered the   as a matter of   I've answered all the questions I'm going to   enough is enough   if you're so   if you're still interested   why don't you take a shot at answering your questions yourself? or get somebody who knows these things   first hand   with experience   don't ask me   just don't ask me   enough is enough   I am not   absolutely not going to   what?   I told you it had already grown dark   not quite dark

Why is it that so much of what you've told me also happens, more or less, in *Isolate Flecks*? *Isolate Flecks*? My God, I haven't thought about that book in years! I remember poor old Leo when it was first published rushing around trying to look as if he wasn't concerned *what* they said about him, the poor unfortunate bastard, as if anybody would have anything at all to say about that wreck, that, I might say *desperate* wreck of a novel. He got *one* review, a terrible one in some rag, I think by that asshole, Vance Whitestone—not that he was wrong about the book—who said something really nasty about the novel being Kaufman's lunge for the main chance. The only thing Leo ever lunged at was somebody's wife's ass—God knows he never got much of his own wife's. Either one. But your question, if you'll forgive me, I think it springs from ignorance—what I mean is you've got it backward. What happens in *Isolate Flecks* is based on what I've told you, it's a *roman à clef*, all the characters in the book are really people Leo knew for years, people I knew for years. A lot of them really blew up when that book was published, you know, the way people do when they think they discover themselves in some book, as if their miserable lives weren't an open book anyway. Pardon the pun. Leo's novel tried to make them look *good*, as a matter of fact. He turned a lot of those deadbeats into artists and poets and such, which Christ knows they weren't. Oh they scribbled and daubed away, dance classes and all the rest of that stupid shit, but they were really concerned with what they used to call making the scene. Even the slang in those days was putrid. There were a few decent ones, by decent I mean somewhat connected to reality, you'll pardon the expression, in some tenuous way. Lou and Sheila Henry, as I've told you already, weren't too bad, nice people really. They were kind of enthralled by that phony bastard Lincoln Gom for a while, with his ecopolitics, and the story goes that he had an affair with Sheila that really ruined Lou for a while, he tried to commit suicide, pills, booze, lost his job, roamed around freeloading, weeping all over his friends, oh Sheila, Sheila, how could you do this to me? You know, really fell apart while Linc was popping the old lady and believe me, Sheila was a luscious piece—Christ, she still looks good now, put on a few pounds with the years but she's still got the most beautiful legs I've ever seen. And a few more were O.K. Lena Schmidt was one—she was engaged for a long time to Anton Harley before he married his wife, Antonia— that's a beauty isn't it? Antonia. Anton and Antonia. That's what's known as a match made in heaven. God what a dummy *she* was! Perfect mate for Anton, sitting around in his corduroys and tweeds with his fucking briars and corncobs and meerschaums spieling away about Proust and Joyce and Christ knows who else, didn't know a damn thing except what he read in the papers, Joe Schmuck's review of the latest novel by one of our ga-rate writers and of course Joe Schmuck is an assistant professor of English at Northeast Boise A and M, talks a lot about characters we care about and moral authority and the artist's obligation to everything and then some. Anyway, how he got hooked up with Lena I'm damned if I know, she was a very nice girl, I think at the time an editorial assistant, she had a slight limp but she was very pretty and sharp. You know that scene in *Isolate Flecks* where the elastic on the girl's panties snaps while she's dancing and they fall down around her ankles? That sort of happened, the girl was Lena and there was a party at Biff Page's house, some rich jerk whose father made Venetian blinds or something, designer shower curtains, I don't know, some great contribution to culture, only Lena didn't *lose* her panties, she was dancing with Anton, I think she'd just met him then and already he was giving her some editorial about the artist's responsibility to communicate and speak to the people and Jack Towne, Jesus, this must have been just about a month or less before he died, Jack Towne, who was drunk, and Lena was in the bag herself a little, Jack yells out, give me a garter of thy love!—I'll always remember that, I think it's from Heine, Rilke maybe, and Lena reached under her skirt and pulled her panties off with a kind of fantastic, I don't know, *elegance*, and threw them across the room. She was absolutely beautiful! Old Anton really got pissed off, he *already* thought that she was his property, you know the type, he probably felt her up and figured that was it. What a pain in the ass he was! Biff, I think, or maybe Chico Zeek, he and Biff worked together in some ad agency or public relations agency or something, but Biff worked for the hell of it, he had an allowance from his old man, anyway, Biff or Chico draped Lena's panties over a lamp in the corner, these tiny little black panties, nothing to them, with a black lace trim. That wasn't a bad party now that I think of it. It went on into the next day, a whole bunch of us after it broke up went to have breakfast in an all-night diner and then we went to the beach, brought a lot of vodka and orange juice and sat around till the sun came up, then we all went back again sloshed to the city to Bunny Lewis's place, Guy, her so-called husband, I think I told you this, he was back again, he and Bunny were always splitting up because Guy had this little business going, a direct-mail business with some grim yokel named Harlan Pungoe and he'd work seven days a week till all hours and was never home. I think he might have been carrying on with a girl who worked for them part-time too, Lorna Flambeaux, she wanted to be a poet, or said she was a poet, some really homely girl she was too, compared to Bunny. But, you know, she must have figured that Guy was going places, as they say, because she worked right alongside him, like a slave, all those horrible hours, and of course Harlan was there too, this hayseed, a good ole boy with a club foot from some damn farm somewhere, I never really liked the guy, there were a lot of creepy stories about him too. Anyway we all, or most of us that had been at Biff's party, got to Bunny's house, wait a minute. Maybe Guy *wasn't* back because Lucy Taylor was there when we all arrived, she'd been there the whole time, I mean she didn't go to the party, and I know that Lucy and Bunny were having a lesbian, let's say, relationship. Lucy was all right, a little mousey, you know how some of those women are, a perfect stereotype really, thick glasses, straight thin hair, stringy you know? and big shapeless breasts, piano legs, and she wore those sweaters, cardigans, and tweed or plaid skirts that came to, you know, mid-calf, the perfect length to make her legs look even worse, flat shoes. A catastrophe. But she was all right and she was pretty good to Bunny, Bunny looked better than ever as a matter of fact, anyway, what the hell was I driving at? Oh right, oh yeah, that was the clincher when it came to Lena and Jack Towne breaking up because Léonie Aubois, *Madame* Aubois, started talking to all kinds of people, oh Christ, she'd been talking all night but she went into high gear that day, swilling down the vodka, what a winner she was, you know the type, she worked at some little boutique that catered to rich women, dumbo celebrities, actresses, so she got to think that this made her important. Anyway, she started to talk to a lot of people and because she hated Lena because Lena wouldn't put up with her pompous crap, she started saying that Lena's taking her panties off was no surprise to *her* because she'd seen some *very* compromising photographs of Lena and two men taken at Horace Rosette's house, pictures that left, as dear Léonie said, nothing to the imagination. So Jack got wind of this and they later, I heard, had a talk about it, and there were harsh words and so on, and Lena refused to deny this picture business, saying that if Jack could even bring it up that was too bad for them both and then good old arts-and-letters Anton moved right in in spades. But it started that day with Léonie talking to anybody who would listen and even those who didn't want to—she was everywhere, lushing up the vodka and buttonholing people, telling them all about these pictures. I remember it as if it happened last week, for Christ sake. I went into the goddam bathroom with Tania Crosse and we smoked a little marijuana to allay the boredom. You could hear Léonie scratching at the door. Pictures! Pictures! Did I tell you about the pictures?

And to whom was Léonie Aubois saying all this?

I told you. To anybody who'd listen to her, when she was into the sauce she'd talk nonstop for hours, days sometimes, and she really developed a kind of mean streak as time went on and by the time she was Madame Aubois, she was a certified bitch. See, she'd worked at this boutique for years, maybe ten, twelve years, and she was still not the manager, the manager was a woman named Sylvie, Sylvie Lacruseille, she was supposed to be French, sure, like my ass is French, the truth of the matter is that Sylvie was the mistress of a very wealthy man, Barnett Tete, who owned boutiques and chic little restaurants and bars and those little stores that sell those little novelties, paper things, you know, you want to buy some goddam napkins for a party and they have these napkins that say Bon Jour or have little notes on them, music, the first couple of bars of a Mozart quartet, all kinds of cutesy things, strictly for the parvenu trade, two-fifty a box of six, you know, and the box is a production as well. Anyway, he had a lot of these places all over as well as, as I said, a few bars, cocktail lounges, authentic English pubs, lots of wood, heavy chairs and tables tastefully scarred, sawdust on the floor for Christ sake, and one place even had brass spittoons, only God forbid that anybody should actually spit in one, they'd call the National Guard. Anyway, Sylvie was Tete's mistress, or one of his mistresses, the one with seniority, let's say, still a good-looking woman the last I saw her, lovely breasts, nice legs, big calves and very slender ankles, very attractive, but as I say, she was no Frenchwoman. The story goes that her name was, well, not even really, but her name was Luba Checks, she came from some steel or mining town, her *real* name was something like Lyubinka Czechowyczy. Tete met her at some hotel bar where she was a cocktail waitress and gave her this name, Sylvie Lacruseille, where he got it I don't know, but I heard that it was from some schlock historical novel about the American Revolution, the real, well, real, you know what I mean, the original fictitious Sylvie Lacruseille was Lafayette's mistress in the book and so on and so forth, the usual tits asses blushes and beauty spots routine. Tete gave her this name and set her up in this boutique into which she came maybe three days a week at most, for a few hours, with a French accent that was so absolutely hilarious that you didn't know whether to shit or go blind when she opened her mouth. She drove away a few customers, not too many though, they didn't know the fucking difference, credit cards and cash and labels they knew. In any event, this really made Léonie more and more sour because she ran the shop, did all the work, even kept the books, did the purchasing, everything, worked ten or twelve hours a day, and to top it all off Tete was sleeping with her whenever he felt like it and she was still the assistant manager, despite Tete's promises. He was a great one with the promises, a shadowy figure as they say, as well, all these fashionable little places were really a sideline, his real money came from some shady deals he had going with some art galleries, art dealers, what, I really don't know, but it had something to do with forgeries, selling them out of the country to collectors, oh not really collectors, nouveau-riche types with money from cocaine and weapons deals who wouldn't know a Picasso from a Braque, and also pulling some deals with prints, you know, printing a thousand and saying that it was a run of a hundred and fifty, the artists signed everything, you know, didn't know a goddam thing, like publishers, you know, who can tell authors they printed three thousand copies of a book when they printed five. But Léonie wasn't always like this, I clearly remember her years before, ten or fifteen years, she had some literary aspirations then as they say, and had even written a novel, not bad really. It was called *The Metal Dress*, I think, but she never got it published. She married a deadbeat, some black jazz musician, Duke Washington, played those weary old be-bop licks and thought he was Charlie Parker. Anyway, to make a long story short, he convinced Léonie that she had no talent and she quit writing, I told her that she really should continue, at least try to get her book published. I knew a guy in those days, Saul Blanche, an editor at what was then a very good house, very adventurous, Crescent and Chattaway, did some good people, Henri Kink, a remarkable poet, and Cecil Tyrell, his novel *Black Hose and Red Heels*, and of course Antony Lamont's *Synthetic Ink*. What was I saying? I told Léonie that I could talk to Saul and have him read her manuscript but she was convinced that this wrong-o, Duke, was right, even though his idea of a book was that it was something you put under the leg of a wobbly table. Well, she and Duke split up eventually, Duke was screwing her best friend and she was working, as I told you, as a cocktail waitress, drinking too much and jumping into bed with the dummies who passed through the hotel, by the time she met Tete she

had no conception of herself as a novelist, she was just on her way to
the Madame Aubois she is now. Well, this scene at Bunny's house, she
was grabbing everybody she could, telling them about these photographs, so-called, of Lena, photographs, by the way, that nobody has
ever seen, but people believed her, some people did anyway, Dick and
April Detective certainly, but that's because they themselves had an,
what shall I say? interest in that sort of thing. April used to send Dick
really steamy pictures of herself when he was on the road, for a while
he was a meat-cutting-machine salesman, and I'll be damned if Dick
didn't show them to people, like, how do you like my wife, sensational,
right? It was very embarrassing and a little, maybe more than a little
sick. So they were delighted to believe this and for months afterward
tried to get ahold of these pictures, they were really a couple of win-
ners. Oh and she talked to a lot of other people, I can't remember all
the people who were there, Leo certainly, and his second wife, Ellen,
they *had* to be there, Leo was writing *Isolate Flecks* at the time and he
was everywhere, gathering material, as he called it, he even had a
little notebook so that he wouldn't lose any really deep thoughts that
came to him when he was away from his beloved desk. And Ellen! I
don't even know what to say about Ellen. She was the kind of woman
who was always talking about cuisine, you know the type, cuisine this
and cuisine that and cuisine the other thing and by Jesus Christ if you
went to their house for a meal you'd get some disaster that you'd turn
down if they gave it to you in the fucking army. The woman would
serve you mashed potatoes, lots of luck, she'd mash them with a goddam fork, all lumps, hopeless. Half-raw carrots, these terrifying sal-
ads with hunks of cheese, my God. Well, they were there for sure, Leo
scribbling away in his little notebook, a little *leather* notebook that
Ellen bought him, you know, like real writers use, to Ellen a real writer
was some guy she saw in a movie, you know, you see this dumb actor
sit down at his typewriter and he types at the top of the page, CHAP-
TER ONE, beautiful! So Léonie knew she had a couple of marks there
and, oh I can't remember all the people there, Biff and Chico, yeah,
and of course Bunny and Lucy, Lucy wouldn't have listened though

because she and Léonie didn't get along to put it mildly. Léonie used to call her Mr. Taylor and ask her what wonderful, what *marrr-velous* Goodwill she bought her clothes at, and Lucy would reply in kind with cracks like how natural Léonie's new hair color looked, such a curious yellow-orange, you'd really have to be right up close to see that it was dyed, oh lots of good clean fun. And as I said, Tania Crosse and I were there, feeling no pain, but the moment we came out of the bathroom we were grabbed by April and Dick, who started to talk and talk to us, unbelievable! They went on and on as if they hadn't seen another human being in ten years.

Well, what was the substance of April and Dick's conversation?

Substance would not exactly be the word. April and Dick were very insubstantial people, but I know what you mean, O.K. As I recall, they wanted to know if I could introduce them to Lena, which was funny, because I'm sure they knew Lena already, but that's what they said they wanted, or maybe I'm thinking of the time we were at Bunny's house after a party at Horace Rosette's? I can't recall exactly, I've known these people so long and they don't ever seem to change, or they change but nothing else does. Anyway. They wanted to meet Lena, I think it was after Biff's party, Tania would remember, but that's neither here nor there, the point is that they said they wanted to meet Lena because they figured that Lena knew Lincoln Gom. As a matter of fact she knew Lincoln all right, they'd been an item as they say, for a year or so, just around the time that Lincoln got involved in his phony ecology and politics dodge. It turned out that it was some kind of scheme having to do with buying up cheap land to make environments or some goddam thing, but what Lincoln really had in mind was building condominiums for rich morons who liked to ski or something, hike, jog, eat cuisine, not smoke, I don't know, healthy things, self-congratulatory things. At this point though, Lena and Lincoln were not speaking to each other, he'd got her involved when they were lovers in working for him as a secretary, Girl Friday, file clerk, the works, in some little dump of an office he opened in Connecticut. The story went that it was funded, that's too fancy a word, I'm beginning to sound like Gom himself, *paid for* is the term, paid for by some guy named Jack Marowitz, Ellen Kaufman's brother, a true hustler who wanted to get in on this condo hustle. Well, Lena moved to Connecticut, which is where, by the way, April and Dick now live, or they did, I should say, until very recently, when they moved up to Vermont, it seems that Connecticut was getting too bourgeois for them, ho ho ho, you understand that I'm talking about people who think that a waiter, for instance, is an inferior being. At any rate Lena moved up to the sticks, she'd really been swept off her feet by Lincoln and his arty friends and she went to work. And I mean work! She did everything, ran the whole office, worked all kinds of hours and half the time she didn't even get paid, can you beat that? So you've got the picture, Lena living with Lincoln, working in his office, you'll pardon the expression, and as likely as not cooking when she got home, cleaning the house, once in a while the sport would take her to a drive-in movie, *I'll Eat Your Eyeballs*, you know, and then buy her a hamburger. Meanwhile he and Marowitz were buying up this land by the fucking fistful and trying to get somebody with *real* money to go in with them on the condo scam, beating the bushes, and then suddenly the deal just fell through. They were informed by the county or the state or somebody that they'd violated some law or ordinance on zoning, or they would if they tried to build, or they wouldn't be able to get a variance or something, so that the whole thing was a bust even if they got the money they needed, which they didn't have a prayer of getting. But Lena didn't know this, there she was, filing and typing these endless letters and one day the so-called business was simply gone and Lincoln and Jack took a powder. There she was alone in Connecticut, and when she got back to town Lincoln was living with what he called an old friend, Rose Zeppole, a girl that everybody called Sister Rose. She'd starred in some porno film playing a nun, I can't remember the name of the thing, *Sisters in Shame*, something like that, anyway she was Sister after that. Which brings me to April and Dick after Horace's party. What they *really* wanted, it turned out, was to meet Lena because of what Léonie had said about the supposed pictures taken at

Horace's, that's right. Lincoln was involved but only because April and Dick had heard that he was making a fortune, along with Marowitz, in the porno racket and they wanted to meet him too. They must have figured that Lena had been in on the beginning of this scheme some years before in Connecticut, since she'd run the office. In other words, they thought that the real-estate business, so called, had never been a real-estate business at all, but a front, from the start, for this little cottage porno-film industry, and that Lena would know about it. When they heard Léonie talking about these photographs of Lena they then thought that Lena was involved on another level as well, right? as a participant. I know that Lena wasn't involved, well, there was nothing to be involved *in*, and that the original scheme was, indeed, a real-estate hustle. The idea that Gom and Marowitz were involved in pornography had no basis in fact. O.K. Rose was living with Lincoln when Lena got back to town and doing, essentially, the same things that Lena had been doing in the country, that is, chief cook and bottle washer, as they say. The Detectives, as I told you, were weird, and they probably wanted to meet other weird people so that they could all be sexually free, you know, group sex, orgies. Or else, who knows, maybe they had ideas about *April* becoming a porno star. I don't know, all I know is that they wanted me and Tania to introduce them to Lena but we told them that Lena was very self-conscious about her slight limp and that it would probably be best to sort of introduce *themselves*, we all played, in other words, our little roles, it was all insane because, as I told you, they knew Lena. And they persisted, they kept at it, until finally it became clear why they wanted us sort of in the middle when they asked us if *we* wanted to go up to their place in Connecticut, yes, they hadn't yet moved further up into God's country. I mean it was just sex, they wanted us and them and Lena to sit around at Bunny's and maybe they'd bring up the photographs or the nonexistent porno business, who knows? To put it bluntly, they wanted to talk dirty, which is why they wanted us involved, the more the merrier. Anyway, they asked us up, Dick started talking about his studio, his studio this, his studio that, it turned out that he had become a photographer, so-

called, I should say he had a lot of equipment. He went to a great deal
of trouble to tell us that he'd studied under, what a glorious phrase,
he'd studied under Annie Flammard, that French-Canadian photographer who made a great splash with photographs of toys? The really
famous one that some big museum bought immediately was that picture of this little old-fashioned wind-up toy, *Tin Pig*. Well, when Dick
said that, with April looking sage and artistic, and the both of them up
to their elbows in filters and shutter speeds and lenses, all that incred-
ibly boring shit that photographers talk about, worse than food freaks,
it occurred to me that Dick was perhaps involved in something unsavory already, because there had been a story about Annie and how
she'd been part of some sort of vice ring or some goddam thing and
she even did some time in Canada. Some weird thing where they'd get
married women, solid citizens, stoned or something and then pose
them in lesbian situations, take pictures, a cheap blackmail scam, but
nobody could ever really find out anything. The gossip was that she
wasn't born Annie Flammard but Roberte Flambeaux, up in some little town either in Canada or right on the Maine border, Christ knows,
a farmer's daughter, no joke, a potato farmer. Anyway, they were really
pushing us to go and visit them, I think they thought that Tania and I
were romantically involved with each other, because April kept running on about a real *fun* weekend with some other *fun* couples, and
they were almost certain that Ted Buckie-Moeller was going to be
there, hallelujah! Ted was a walking wet dream, also a photographer,
a fashion photographer I think, and his great claim to fame, outside of
the wild rumor that he once got a model to speak a declarative sentence of more than four words, was that his place was featured in some
magazine as being an example of Now Living. He lived in a loft that
had no furniture, no books, no pictures, nothing but a big barn of a
place with about five hundred fucking pillows on the floor, one whole
wall a movie or TV screen and another filled with a huge collection of
cigarettes, packs of cigarettes. A deep thinker. So at that moment, over
the din of Léonie and Lucy sweetly murdering each other and the
melodious sound of vodka being guzzled by the gallon, I heard a little

voice, that of my guardian angel, saying, these people are fucking id-
iots. Anyway, Tania escaped, just went back into the bathroom. I really
envy the way women can escape to the bathroom. When I started to
move into the living room, edge my way in, they were right with me
and I guess that the sacred name of Buckie-Moeller hadn't given my
face enough of a look of wild anticipation, because they started to tell
me that Vance Whitestone would also probably come up to the old
barn—they called their place in the woods the old barn—isn't that too
fucking sweet? Yes, Vance would be up with Karen Ostrom, his then-
current inamorata, who was, I think, an airline stewardess. Maybe
even—ruffle of drums!—Lincoln Gom would be there! I had a fleeting
vision of the *Garden of Earthly Delights*. So I said that it looked pretty
good for me, they should call. All the time I'm thinking of an opening
I'd gone to about three years earlier, maybe four years? of photographs
by none other than Annie Flammard, and then a wonderful conversation that those same three—Vance, Karen, and Lincoln—had in a
bar that they went to, that a lot of us went to, after the show. I was in a
booth right behind them with Marcie Butler, who was just in the pro-
cess of splitting up with Saul Blanche, who'd suddenly discovered that
he was in reality a homosexual, and I got an earful.

What did Whitestone, Gom, and Miss Ostrom talk about in the
bar to which they went afterward?

Well, when these three got together it was murder in the henhouse, they were vicious gossips, the slightest rumor became fact with
them, really made for each other. The funniest thing about it all was
that at this time, with Karen living with Vance, she was also getting a
little on the side from Linc, who was also having an affair with Bart
Kahane's wife, Lolita—or it might have been with his ex-wife, Conchita, that's terrific, isn't it? Lolita and Conchita, almost as good as
Anton and Antonia, I can't imagine where these people got these
names, not to mention the Detectives, of course, but there they are.
Anyway, Lincoln thought he was pulling a fast one on both Lolita, it
must have been Lolita because Conchita was then in Europe, France
I think, when Annie had her opening, so, Lincoln thought he was pull-

ing a fast one on Lolita and his good pal, Vance, not to mention Bart, but the truth of the matter was that Vance knew all about it and was delighted, because when Karen was with Lincoln she, of course, couldn't be with him. Which is exactly what he wanted because Karen was getting on his nerves, as well she might, might get on anyone's nerves, you know the type, wheat germ and black-strap molasses and raw milk with the yoga and the courses in adult education, you'll pardon the expression, How to Order Wine, Keep Fit, Write and Be Happy, Getting the Most Out of Your Leotard, you know the kind of thing I mean, plus all that mystical shit about smoking a little goddam pedestrian joint. Used to read books about the correct way to eat spaghetti, for Christ sake. She was getting on Lincoln's nerves too, truth to tell, but she had bread, a good salary, you know, and this was just about the time that Linc was trying to hustle the real-estate deal with Marowitz. But you want to know what they were talking about, O.K. This really places them beautifully. A few months earlier, Cecil Tyrell, no, that was later, I don't know how I could have confused it, I mean to say Lamont, a few months earlier Antony Lamont published his novel, *Synthetic Ink*, it came out from, as I told you, Crescent and Chattaway, C and C, as people called it. Tony had published earlier books— let's see, one was *Rayon Violet*, another one was called, I think, *Baltimore Chop*, they both got crucified, but then slowly he started to get a reputation, Saul Blanche went to the wall for him at C and C, and they took his new book, *Synthetic Ink*. O.K., now you have to realize that this was a break for Tony, if the book did pretty well, broke even anyway, the chances were that maybe he'd have a publisher for his next book, of course there was no next book and there probably won't be, I mean it's been almost fifteen years since then and Tony is a dedicated drunk, always starting his really *great* novel, hopeless. Anyway, where was I? Anyway, right, *Ink* comes out and the first review it gets is in a rag, a weekly, called *Hip Vox* as a matter of fact, exactly the kind of garbage that somebody like Karen would read like the bible, what to eat, where to go, what movies are good, they discovered writers and painters, Jesus, guys who should have been left under a rock, you

know what I mean? As a matter of fact, Karen *did* read this crap, goddam thing filled with ads selling you a pair of used combat boots for
eighty bucks, foolishness. Anyway, it gets this big, *big* review, a picture
of Tony, must have been twenty-five hundred words, the featured ar-
ticle, and on the front page a little banner across the top says something like Lamont's Ink Not Permanent, some cutesy catchy shit like
that, and here's this review by some ace, Christ-all knew who he was,
a guy named John Hicks. Who? everybody said, not least of all Tony
and Saul, you better believe it. Anyway, it was one of the most savage,
vicious reviews I've ever seen, Lamont wound up looking as if he was
a rapist, child molester, fascist, misogynist, you name it, all rolled into
one, plus of course the worst writer since God knows who, Page Moses
maybe. He got a couple of reasonably good reviews after that but they
came too late to do any good, and they were too small, you know, nobody saw them, besides, the fashionable readers of *Hip Vox* stayed
away from the book in droves, it was, right? not *hip* to read it! So the
usual, no sales, lots of returns, the book was eventually pulped because no remainder outfit would buy it for a price that C and C could
swallow, and Saul even had to quit C and C finally, they started to give
him real dogs to work on, *Jog Your Way to Orgasm*, really, that was a
book, and that was that, the well-known handwriting was on the wall,
everybody was walking around wondering who in the name of Christ
this guy, John Hicks, was. Léonie Aubois, I've got to give her credit
because she smelled a rat, said it was probably a phony monicker for
Vance Whitestone, and damn if she wasn't close, I'll get to that. So I'm
sitting in the booth with Marcie, wait a minute. I should tell you some,
give you some background to this stuff so you'll be able to understand
the ins and outs of it all. When Vance first came on the scene he was a
poet of sorts, and sorts, believe me, covered a lot of territory, he was
really *bad*, mediocre, worse than mediocre. I mean he was what you
could call rotten. Craig Garf, who's involved now in television commercials, I'll be damned if I know what he does, arranges corn flakes,
some imbecile shit, Craig at that time had a little magazine going, I
can't remember the name of it, it was filled with these hopeless little

poems, looked like they came out of some computer programmed by a moron, these poems that trot down the page one word to a line and go something like, oh I don't know, you know what I mean, the sun is gold and your moonhair shines, some shit like that, one word to a line, all small letters, really *modern* in nineteen twenty-five. Anyway, Craig was on the hustle, trying to make a name for himself as a very revolutionary poet and editor with this little piece of, oh right, *Lorzu* was the name of it, and, well, I bring this up because Vance couldn't even get into *this* magazine. But then he started to go to Horace Rosette's, Horace was at the time a psychiatric social worker or some useless goddam thing, a clerk at the unemployment office, too good, of course of *course*, for the job, but he was very much the lover of art. By that I mean that he befriended young writers and painters, preferably good-looking young guys. Dear Horace would have them over for private poetry readings that would end up most of the time in Horace's bed. He even went occasionally for girls if they looked like boys, once in a while couples, that's neither here nor there. He had a lot of parties, lots of booze and food, actual *food*, not a few slices of American cheese and a box of crackers. What was I saying? Vance started to go to Horace's, became part of the gang, more like a coven, and his star, as they say, started to rise, because Horace got Craig's ear and told him that though Vance didn't have that *something* that makes for the poetic temperament, he had a great deal of, how did Horace put it? oh, yes, critical acuity, sure he did, which meant simply that Horace was blowing him like a trumpet and taking it up the old wazoo. Anyway, Craig knew, as they say, which side his bread was buttered on, and Vance suddenly started writing these haughty little reviews for *Lorzu*. In the meantime, Vance met Anne Kaufman at a party at Horace's, Anne and Leo were having a lot of trouble at the time, the marriage was breaking up, they'd got married right after they both graduated college, playing house, you know, living in some grim furnished apartment while Anne went out to work. Leo was collecting rejection slips and getting swacked every other day, this went on and on till finally they just sort of tolerated each other and Anne was looking to fool around.

Leo couldn't get it up anymore anyway unless, so the story goes, but who knows? unless he could first undress Anne and then spank her. She wasn't having any too much of this. Anyway, Anne met Vance Whitestone, fanfare! critic, at one of Horace's parties and they began an affair, she was impressed because Vance's reviews began to appear here and there outside of *Lorzu* and he got a teaching job somewhere, creative writing, what else? and about a dozen people knew his name. She was also impressed because, Jesus! Vance was one of those corny bastards with the walks in the rain, the little Greek restaurants that he'd found up some alley and down in a cellar, ferry rides, tweeds and corduroys and work shirts, all he needed was some big goddam fucking dog crapped out at his feet. So this went on for a while, a year, year and a half, meanwhile Anne and Leo got a divorce. Leo then walked around crying all over everyone, playing soppy songs on the jukebox, *Are You Lonesome Tonight?*, drinking boilermakers like water, and living with one old friend after another, how could you turn him down, the pathetic bastard. Then, into this idyllic amour of Anne and Vance's came, organ chord! none other than the well-known cult-coterie-raffiné author, Antony Lamont, and in a trice, as Vance might say when he coins a cliché, in a trice, Tony was in Anne's pants. The problem was that everybody knew what was going on except Vance, the son of a bitch was so wrapped up in himself and his dumb literary *career* that it never occurred to him that Anne might give him a set of horns. When he found out he went apeshit, as they used to say, had a fight with Tony, who casually gave him a black eye, and then went home and took Anne's dresses, those she still had at his place, and cut them up with a scissors. A lot of class. So when *Ink* was published and got the bejesus kicked out of it in *Hip Vox*, we were surprised that it wasn't Vance in a way, but in another way not, because he was probably still afraid that Tony would kick his ass for him again. Which brings me back to Léonie's idea that maybe John Hicks was just a phony name for Vance, but she found out from somebody, some guy who worked at *Hip Vox*, that this guy John Hicks was the McCoy. So there I am in the bar with Marcie, she's telling me a lot of embarrassing things about her sex life with Saul, what he liked to do and how he liked to do it, this and that, no need to go into it, but she figured she should have suspected that he was twisted because of these kinks, and I'm listening and telling her that she shouldn't mind, after all they can still be friends, I'm beginning to sound to myself like the proverbial man with a paper asshole, or like Horace Rosette when he's coming on to some college freshman, Horace would quote yards of Elizabeth Barrett Browning and Rupert Brooke, for Christ sake. Anyway. With my other ear I'm hearing Lincoln, Vance, and Karen in the next booth. Karen says, well you finally got even with Leo after all this time, oh, I forgot to tell you that Leo told everybody that when Anne and Vance started in, Vance pressured Anne to take all of her and Leo's money, maybe a couple of grand, out of their joint savings account and she did. So Leo told *everyone* this story, he was quite a weeper in his day, anyway, Karen says this, she was talking of course about Vance's shot at *Isolate Flecks*, and this brings on a lot of laughs, and then, aha, Lincoln says, yes, it *was* sweet, but it lacked the beauty of the Hicks job, so I'm immediately all ears, meanwhile Marcie is telling me about Saul and Christ knows what all, bowls of milk and raw eggs, cross-dressing, golden showers, I don't know, like French porn, I don't remember because I'm really *listening* to Lincoln and Vance. To make it short it turns out that this guy John Hicks was a student of Vance's and he got him this job doing the review of *Synthetic Ink*, his actual name in actual print! It was, of course, understood that Hicks would tear Tony's book to shreds. Then, later on, a few months, maybe only a month, I found out from Lucy Taylor, when she was staying for a while at Lou and Sheila's place, that's a story in itself, by the way, I found out from Lucy why the editor of *Hip Vox*, who was a woman, Lee Jefferson, why she let Vance talk her into letting this kid, John Hicks, do a review, just like *that*. That had really seemed strange to me because Lee used to work and pal around with Saul at C and C.

What's that about Lucy Taylor at Lou and Sheila's?

Did I say Lou and Sheila's? I meant to say Leo and Ellen's that Lucy stayed at or, now wait a minute, it could have been, at that time,

Leo and Anne's. I should make it clear that while Leo's marriage with Anne was breaking up and she was seeing, *seeing*, terrific word, Vance, Leo had already started carrying on with the future Mrs. Kaufman, Ellen, who, by the way, I maybe forgot to mention was Jack Marowitz's younger sister? In any event, Leo and Anne still had their apartment although they were rarely in it at the same time, Anne, as a matter of fact, had moved in, in effect, with Vance, and Leo was with Ellen as much as he could be, sniffing around her skirts, mooning over her, for Christ sake, well why not? She let him spank her and he ate her yogurt and wild grass. The perfect couple. In any case, Lucy stayed with the Kaufmans, but I just can't recall now if Ellen had already become Leo's wife at the time. Christ, Lucy wouldn't have stayed with Lou and Sheila if *not* to meant sleeping in the park. She hated them with a passion. But she got along fine with Leo, probably felt sorry for the pitiful bastard.

Why did Leo Kaufman leave Rosette's with Anne instead of Ellen?

Oh, that was the famous night that Horace gave a party for Bart because he'd just got a nice fat check from some jerk he did a doctoral dissertation for. Bart was part of a group of people who used to write theses and dissertations and such for grad students mostly, and Bart had done this paper on math for somebody who didn't know his ass from his elbow, I can't remember the paper, it's not important, something about complex resolutions or contravariant resolutions, whatever, anyway, anyway, as I've told you, Horace loved to give parties. He might well have had his eye on Bart at that time, I don't know, Bart wasn't artistic, as they say, and that was always Horace's weakness. Annie Flammard was there, she'd just married Barry Gatto who was, of all things, a piano tuner which was delicious because the son of a bitch had an ear made of pure tin, but he had a great line of jive and had some kind of a partnership with a girl by the name of Buffie, Buffie Tate, who was an interior decorator, she called it a space-décor consultant, some kind of bunk. Barry would go into somebody's house to tune the piano, God help the poor bastards, and while he was there, he was lovely, he had this fake Italian accent, you know? While he was there tuning and tinkering, butchering the damn piano, he'd start talking about how ver' nize it would be if the lady of the howze she's a put a white-a velvet couch here an' oh si, thees wall-a is perfect to have some shelves with little drawings, and on and on and then he'd recommend his fren', Mizz Tate, oh si, why Mizz Tate had consulted for the most wonderful and chic and rich people in the most wonderful houses and maybe ten percent of the time he'd land some fish and Buffie would be in business. They had some kind of sliding percentage deal depending on how much Buffie could squeeze out of the marks. Anyway, he married Annie Flammard, she was still a painter then, or maybe she was making sculpture, I don't clearly remember, purely a business arrangement. Buffie and Barry and Annie formed this trium-virate, right? Barry would set up the mark, Buffie would come in and consult, and then guess who she'd recommend as a fantastic artist, not really big *yet*, but on the verge, oh yes, *absolutely* the time to buy her for those who are truly *au courant*, for those who could spot some-one who was going to be one of the hottest, in-demand painters in the country in a few years, her prices were insanely low, but she had to eat, Buffie felt in a way that perhaps she was even, well, taking advan-tage of a great artist but, well, the client had been so wonderful, she felt really *close* to her, the apartment or house had come to seem like Buffie's own, it was none other than, yes, Annie Flammard! A young vibrant Parisian artist who had come to America because things were so *exciting* here! Enter Annie, trotting out another phony accent, black boots and black tights, turtleneck, Gitanes, and she'd have the mark in for a private, *exclusive* showing and unload a half a dozen things on her, Christ knows what, on some of them the fucking paint was still wet. It was a sweet little deal and they ultimately had a going *ménage à trois*, business with pleasure, as they say. So they were at Horace's and a lot of other people, Bart and Conchita, Lolita, that was the night that Bart and Lolita met the Henrys as a matter of fact, Page Moses, the worst writer the world has ever known, we used to call him Doctor Plot, what a case, and some joker who worked in the same place as

Biff Page and Chico, I think his name was, amazingly enough, Sol Blanc, not to be confused with Saul Blanche, but to tell the truth, it was uncanny how much they resembled each other. I think even Jack Marowitz came that night, he wanted to meet his sister's husband, Leo, he was a little put out because they didn't have a religious ceremony when they got married, he was very big on that religious idea, he wanted to take a look at this deadbeat who'd married his beloved sister. They were of course there, Leo and Ellen, I remember unfortunately as if it were yesterday Ellen's zucchini cake and her kohlrabi quiche, she'd brought them to help out, Jesus Christ almighty! If you put them in a gun you could sink a battleship with them. Lincoln Gom, oh right, with Sister Rose, Rose Zeppole, who at the time was modeling lingerie in a showroom for department store buyers and paying the rent for Lincoln, who was *into*, as they now put it, radical politics then, he'd stand around talking about the struggle of the peoples and the bourgeois canon and running dogs of imperialism, sweet Jesus, meanwhile Rose was fighting off these guys from the vast heartland and doing a few small favors for some of them, right? all in a day's work. Lena was there too, and in very bad shape, Jack Towne had died about a month before from booze and pills, in a way it was inevitable, he'd been heading for it for a long time, but it was bitter, bitter, you couldn't find a sweeter guy than Jack. The story that went around was that he'd really been crushed because of the pictures that had supposedly been taken of Lena and then their quarrel about it. As a matter of fact his death, and it was really suicide however you want to slice it, his death had assured everybody that the pictures, you know, that they actually existed and that Jack couldn't handle it. However. Well. However, this wasn't the truth. The truth was that Jack had got himself tangled up in some mess concerning a nursing home, I think I mentioned that he was some kind of supervisor or inspector for the city? Something to do with housing preservation and urban renewal, something, and he O.K.'d some old-age home that had violations or whatever. To make a long story short, the place was unsafe and he and some sleazy bastard who used the name Biggs Richard, there's a fake handle

for you, Jack and this guy Richard made a deal on some kind of doc-
tored report on this place, for money of course, I mean Jack got money
from this guy, I don't know how much but a nice taste, and I don't know
the ins and outs of it but that creepy yokel, Harlan Pungoe, was somehow at the bottom of it, he stood to make a real bundle. So what happened is that the goddam second floor of the place collapsed and seven
old people were killed, a lot were badly hurt, a nurse was killed, and
Jack was left holding the bag. This guy Richard was somehow con-
veniently in the clear, and Pungoe was, as they say, not connected in
any way. So Jack started to, well, kill himself, by degrees, and whether
it was because he knew that the investigation that the city started
would absolutely destroy him, or land him in jail, or it was simply the
guilt over these dead people, or all three things, anyway, that was it.
He did kill himself. But I'm way off your question about Leo and Anne,
right? Sorry. O.K. Leo and Ellen came and they were there about an
hour when in walks Anne, she looked like a million wearing this
knockout of a shift dress in off-white raw silk, she'd gained a *little*
weight in, as they say, the right places. The only woman at the party
better looking than Anne was Marcie Butler, but she was something
really special, she had the most beautiful legs I've ever seen. Well,
Anne and Ellen and Leo started to talk, you know, the old civilized
routine, and I guess that Anne had had a few too many on the way,
whatever, but she started in about Leo's sexual, ah, proclivities? shall
I say? Well, Ellen was enormously embarrassed and of course there's
big brother Jack, looking at this weird son of a bitch who, Jack must
have thought, was running his kid sister through some heavy sadomasochist routine. There were words, and Ellen demanded that Leo
tell Anne off, and Anne said something about well, whatever else Leo
was when *we* were married, he certainly was not henpecked, and
what was the matter with Ellen that she was angry about Leo's first
marriage, was she maybe insecure? Jack Marowitz got in on it, with
sick Leo, disgusting Leo, spineless Leo, and Anne suddenly just
grabbed Leo by the arm and bang! out the door they went. None of us
quite knew what to do, we tried to treat it like a joke, or not exactly

that, but we tried to make light of it as they say, a lot of loud talk, you know, and forced hearty laughter. Except for the other people who were at Horace's, who at that time were always in a little group by themselves, like a little cabal, they hardly paid any attention to what was going on. A spooky bunch.

What other people at Horace Rosette's?

Well, as I said, this little cabal, if that's the word, a kind of informal club, I suppose, kindred spirits, as I say, spooky, if that's not too melodramatic a word. Guy Lewis with his employer and friend, if you will, that good ole boy, Harlan Pungoe, some creep named Roger Whytte-Blorenge, which is a wonderful handle, except when you met the guy his accent was strictly Joizy Cidy, you know what I mean? You'd be introduced to this guy, this is Mr. Whytte-Blorenge, Roger Whytte-Blorenge, and he'd say, you know, pleeztameecha, scuze me I gotta gota duh terlet. Beautiful. All I knew about him is that he worked for Pungoe, or had worked for him, anyway, they'd known each other for years, he was a kind of gofer, there was something really weird about him, he'd get a few in him or smoke a little hash and the next thing you know he'd be sitting in front of some woman, sitting on the floor, and staring at her shoes. And let's see, the rest of the good old gang, Lorna Flambeaux, who insisted that she was Annie Flammard's sister, but Annie denied it, said she'd never even seen her till, say, maybe two years before, when she first arrived in town. Lorna worked at the time as a first reader for some publishing house, I don't remember which one, and she was, I believe, romantically involved with Roger, which is a thought that still astounds me, I can just see them getting into their apartment and Roger making a dive for her feet, oh yes, as I told you, Lorna had ambitions to be a poet, she had some crackpot theory that Sade was a woman or something like that, and was writing a cycle of poems, or an epic poem, her idea was that Sade was, Christ, I don't know, that he was really his wife, and the man, the Marquis de Sade, was some pure and innocent sap who took the fall for her, the true writer of the books, the real libertine. Anyway that's what her poem was about, so I heard. She said that only a woman could think up all those perversions, or as she put it, those *marvelous* perversions. And oh yes, of course, there was another woman, Annette Lorpailleur, I don't know *what* to tell you about her. There was something, what's the word? something really nasty, unsavory about her, she was quite beautiful, somehow regal-looking, but something, something about her. She was thought to be a kind of partner with Harlan in his direct-mail business, some offshoot of it anyway, but nobody ever really knew what the offshoot or whatever you want to call it, was. My own idea, that I came to from, well, let's say this and that, is that it had something to do with, I don't know exactly, but some sort of religious cult or something, not really *religious*, I don't know. Something to do with the occult, some sort of magic, probably all crap anyway, but the money came rolling in, so I heard, they had members or devotees, initiates, all over the country, all over the world I think, some sort of orgiastic thing going, satanism, I know one thing and that's that Guy Lewis was absolutely smitten with her, he was, if you'll forgive me, bewitched. There was something really chilling about her, distant, her voice, well, her *voice*. The way she talked, it wasn't as if she had an accent or anything, it was as if her voice wasn't exactly coming from *her*—you know, as if somebody was talking and she was moving her mouth in this funny stiff way, just like, well, just like a ventriloquist's dummy. That was the group, a real fun bunch, and there were two other women, no, they came on the scene about a year later, by that time Guy was going home just to change his clothes so to speak. Right, they came later, two women who moved in with Annette, Corrie Corriendo and a Madame Delamode, I don't know what her first name was, but they weren't at this particular party, as I say. I should correct myself by the way, they didn't move in with Annette, the three of them bought a huge co-op apartment and had it completely redone, completely decorated to their taste. It was an absolutely incredible place, sumptuous, strange and sumptuous. It must have cost them a mint.

You referred to some paper of agreement or contract that Lou signed with or for Saul Blanche—what was that all about?

Right. It wasn't a contract *per se*, in a sense it was a gentlemen's agreement, but there was a written something or other that Lou signed, yes. Lou and Sheila, Lou mostly but Sheila was also interested, Lou got her interested, were bibliophiles, book collectors, you know, especially interested in modern first editions, manuscripts, letters, notebooks, and they were as they say devoted and quite knowledge-able—not just the usual thing, I mean they didn't try to get hold of, acquire stuff done by only well-known writers. They were also, or I should say they were *primarily* interested in writers whose reputa-tions were just beginning, it was more interesting Lou once said, more risky and exciting, you know, the idea being that he was, or they were, taking a chance on writers who might fail or disappear, just fold up. Of course it was much cheaper too and they didn't have a hell of a lot of money, they both worked, you know, just ordinary people. Well, Saul, as an editor at C and C, C and C being a house that published a lot of avant-garde, experimental fiction and poetry in those days, those days however being gone forever—now they do the same weary stuff that everybody else does, novels that could have been written two hundred years ago, *angst* at the pool among the sensitive young in a world they don't understand, or how the TV repairman talked so funny because his wife ran away with the motel manager. Christ, they even published a novel by good old Doctor Plot, I mean here was a scribbler that even vanity presses used to run screaming into the night from. That's not the point. The point is that in those days C and C was different and Saul, being an editor, would see an awful lot of manuscripts, a lot of them were rejected, good stuff too, it's just that they couldn't do every-thing and a lot of it was too difficult, as they say, and written by writers with tiny reputations, no audience, they couldn't afford the losses, but Saul would know or take an educated guess, you know, that these were writers who would some day be important. Well, he and Lou made a deal that, with an author's consent, Lou could buy the manuscript, the original manuscript, and Saul would get a cut and give the author a cut of his cut, and he'd do this with manuscripts that the house had turned down. I suppose that maybe it could be viewed as exploitation but on the other hand the author gave his consent and could always copy the original, probably had copies anyway. Most often Saul would ask the author for the rough draft, the working manuscript, which, of course, Lou would be most interested in. As I say, it could be seen as exploitation but it kept a lot of writers eating, as a matter of fact, Cecil Tyrell's first novel, that was turned down by C and C, was sold—in this case, the whole thing, I mean the typescript, working drafts, note-books—just like this. Saul had read it and got in touch with Lou and Cecil said, hell, all right, so Lou has all that material. As a matter of fact he's even talked about maybe publishing it for Cecil himself, you know, privately, because Cecil hasn't ever found a publisher for it, I can't remember the title, I think it's *Orange Steel*. It's supposed to be very difficult, what's the word, inaccessible. Sheila said that Cecil told her that he took the three classical unities, or I should say he took two of the classical unities and discarded them so that the book has no action and no time, only place, or no action and no place, only time, or something, and the element, the unity that's left is presented as a cat-alogue. It's just one long list or a series of lists. In any event that's the nature, that was the nature of the agreement. I don't think it's in force anymore, Saul is long gone from C and C. To tell you the truth, though, Lolita Kahane was really angry about the *Orange Steel* business and even called Sheila up about it, and from what I know it wasn't a very friendly conversation.

And what did Lolita have to say to Sheila on the telephone?

It's funny to think about this, it was so many years ago, we were all pretty young, I doubt if Lolita would even remember it now, Jack Towne was still very much alive, Sheila and Lou were still married, Horace hadn't taken his act, so to speak, to France. It was amazing by the way, how he left, Christ only knows where he got the money but he got it, the story was confused, something about money being em-bezzled by Léonie Aubois, but nobody ever proved anything, the money was probably dirty money anyway, you know what I mean? Money that couldn't be reported as stolen because it wasn't supposed to exist in the first place. Well you don't need all this, it just struck me thinking about Sheila and Lolita when they were young women. As I remember, Lolita had lived with Cecil the whole time he was writing *Orange Steel,* and he was some number in those days, to call him a fucking disgusting boor would be a *little* too kind, drinking, I mean falling-down drinking, a foul and vicious mouth, he'd hit people, mostly women, mostly, of course, Lolita. It was a godsend really for her when Cecil took a powder and she met Bart, who was, despite his being a con man and a bullshit artist, a reasonable human being. But she'd lived with Cecil and paid all the bills all the time he was working on this book, it's not a very big book but it took him more than three years to write. Anyway she knew all about Lou and Sheila and their collecting, and as far as she was concerned they were simply thieves. I think she used to call them the vultures. Besides, she hated Saul Blanche because he walked right in on her, on purpose, you know? when she was in the bathroom at one of Horace's parties, and he caught her in a very embarrassing position, you know, and then he had the nerve to, this is according to Lolita, he had the nerve to stand there and watch her, just stand there smoking a cigarette. So she had no love for any of them. On top of this it's a cinch that she also knew that those nights that Cecil didn't come home, or I should say, crawl home, were spent with, not all of them but a lot of them, they were spent with Sheila, and with the knowledge, even the assistance, the connivance of Lou. I mean, an awful lot of people knew about this oddball activity that was going down and Lolita must have heard it from somebody, if from no one else then from Léonie, who was always the official mouth, believe it! This would have been bad enough but it was clear, or it became clear to Lolita that all these sex games had to do with something else, what, I don't know, but something to do with this novel that Cecil was working on, who knows? Maybe the Henrys were already convincing Cecil that they'd love to buy his manuscript, I don't know. Well when the book was finished and turned down by C and C and then a few other houses, that's when Saul arranged for the sale and so on as I've already told you, and Lolita called Sheila up and told her what she thought of her and of Lou too, of course. Cecil had taken his share of the sale money and poured it down his throat, and with some of it he gave the business to Barnett Tete, I mean to say that he and Sylvie took off for a week or ten days together, which is about the time, or I should say that because of this fling, Barnett kicked Sylvie's ass out of the boutique, but he still didn't make Léonie the manager, which did not, as you can imagine, make her disposition any sweeter. Instead, Barnett asked Tania if she wanted to be the manager, Tania Crosse, and she accepted, same deal as with Sylvie—she didn't turn a hand, came in when she goddam well pleased, and bought the most expensive clothes at forty, fifty percent off. In addition, of course, to the ones Tete bought for her because to be Tete's manager was to be his mistress. Or one of them. Well, all this is neither here nor there, but I should add that Tania, who is now known as Madame LaCrosse, is always in some goddam magazine or other, the successful businesswoman, you know the sort of nauseating set-pieces they do, glamorous, chic, elegant Madame LaCrosse is also one of the fashion world's most hardworking and hardheaded business executives, then there's a picture spread, Tania on the beach, Tania climbing a snow-capped mountain, Tania consulting with her staff, Tania giving a crippled kid some dumb plaque, Tania smiling at the mayor or some other fucking idiot, and then a little sanitized interview-story about the rewards of the fashion game for women bent on exciting careers, enough to make you puke on your shoes. Anyway, I wanted to tell you that all this began for her when Barnett took her out of the boutique and opened yet another one, a specialty shop, for her. She must have really rung old Tete's bells for him, hauled his ashes *good*. It was a little overpoweringly snobbish trap, obscenely expensive, that dealt only in what they called ultra-intimate apparel, the usual lingerie, but *very* expensive, and then a special line of kinky stuff, French and Italian, made of the most expensive materials, the shop was called, beautiful! Soirée Intime. A wardrobe of their ultra-intimate apparel, as their demurely suggestive ads said, color-coordinated—color spelled with a u—color-coordinated for those magic moments after midnight, a wardrobe of this stuff cost enough to keep a large family eating for a year. Anyway, this is far off Lolita's phone call, but you know you get to thinking about all this after so many years, if anyone ever asked Tania if she'd like to share a joint in the bathroom nowadays she'd probably turn her three Nazi dobermans loose. That day seems as if it happened a century ago.

Why did John Hicks visit Horace Rosette some time after the party had broken up?

Well, wait a second, the party, there were so many parties at Horace's and other places that I don't know exactly what party you mean. But John Hicks, the famous iconoclastic book reviewer, he was only around for about a year and a half, a little less, then he just disappeared. As a matter of fact he disappeared about the same time that Henri Kink did, right after Henri's novel, his one and only novel, was published, so I think I know just about the time you mean, although Christ knows he might have gone to see dear old Horace every night as far as I know. Anyway, the time you mean is pretty much common knowledge because Horace dropped hints about it, hints the man says, he talked about it *incessantly* to everybody because he said that Hicks was so nervous, not nervous, Horace's word was terrified, Hicks was so terrified, he said, that he was really worried when he just disappeared into, as they say, thin air. Anyway, he talked about it all the time and it must have been, as I said, right about the same time that Henri's novel, *Mouth of Steel* was its title, was published. The book, by the way, had what they call an interesting history. It was written in English but Henri couldn't find a publisher and so it was originally, God knows how, originally published for the first time in France, in a French translation, as *La Bouche métallique*, and created a little stir over there. I'll be damned if it wasn't then published here, by Beaumont and Halpin, in English—only for some weird reason the original English text *wasn't* published. The version that appeared here was a translation of the French translation back into English. Anyway, that's neither here nor there, except that there was a rumor that the translator, somebody named Anthony Octavio, whom nobody ever heard of and never has since, was really Sol Blanc, though that seems far-fetched to me because the only thing French that fat Sol knew anything about was French fries. Besides, he had a hell of a lot of trouble speaking English, he was some kind of a refugee or some goddam thing, came over as an exchange student or I don't know what, whoever sent him didn't want him back, not that I'd blame them. But you want to know about why John Hicks went to Horace's after the party that we've got, I think, straight, which one or which time. I hope I can remember this, it was about, let's see, *Mouth of Steel* came out about, well, I guess six or seven years ago so it was that long ago, O.K. What I heard is that Hicks went to see Horace because he was up to his ears in some very shady goings-on with Annette Lorpailleur and her two cronies I told you about, Corrie Corriendo and Madame Delamode, who were all, at this time, living in this dazzling apartment I mentioned, well, *dazzling*, yes, but not in any warm, bright way, very strange and icy to tell you the truth. The whole place was sinister. John Hicks wanted out from under Annette and the other two women, it seems that he told Horace some strange stories about weird rites of some sort, sex orgies with all kinds of people, he was involved with all of it, along with, as far as my own opinion goes, along with that loathsome rube, Pungoe, Mr. Congeniality. What Hicks wanted was for Horace to give him some money or talk to somebody for him or something at the place he worked, I told you that Horace was some kind of sociopsychological something, I think, but Horace really didn't know exactly *what* he wanted, or so he said. You can bet your ass that Horace wasn't about to give anybody any of the old mazoo, not Horace. To him every buck that he had left after he paid the rent and etcetera went for a party, or for entertaining, shall I say? his interesting and artistic young friends, man, woman, or animal. Anyway, to be as brief as I can, it got around after Hicks disappeared that he was no young Lochinvar who'd shown up all sparkling eyes and hot breath in Vance's writing class, out of the woods with mud on his boots and egg on his vest, no, it turned out that Star Eyes was Pungoe's *contact* with this guy Biggs Richard in the nursing-home swindle I mentioned earlier. As a matter of fact, since nobody on God's earth had ever laid eyes on Biggs Richard a lot of people put two and two together and had it figured that they were the same guy, I mean Hicks and Richard. Now that I think of it I remember that Jack Towne told me that when he was involved with Richard—except that he never told me what for—that he never could *meet* the man, they did everything over the phone, which was, I'm sure, true, only as I say Jack never told me what it was all about, just ran some story down to me about it all being some kind of a quick-buck scheme having to do with selling a goddam whole warehouse full of some kind of synthetic-metal fabric that garment makers use for those, you know, those shiny metallic gowns and costumes, show-biz tuxedoes, you know the stuff I mean, but I never thought twice about it since Jack was always trying to make a fast score one way or another. Anyway. Where was I? Right, right, Hicks wanted out of whatever he was involved in and, as I said, Horace said that he was absolutely shaking with fear, take Horace's descriptions with a grain of salt, O.K., but he was impressed and had no reason to make it all up, and Horace said that Hicks left his place without saying in any clear way what it exactly was that was spooking him, then he was suddenly missing, I mean he simply *vanished*. Vance went to check on him after he hadn't been able to get him on the phone for more than a week and there was his place, intact, everything in it, books and records, clothes, food in the refrigerator, an open pack of cigarettes on the table, just as if he'd gone down the block for a bottle or a loaf of bread, he was just gone. On the kitchen table there's a sheet of paper, Vance just left it there, he said that it gave him a chill just to look at it. On the paper there were, I don't know, odds and ends of writing or something, calligraphy, more like little drawings, I really don't know, circles and pentagrams and bits of Greek or Hebrew or some damn thing, runes, and that was it. Vance said the phone rang while he was there and he almost jumped out of his skin. It's funny you should ask this question because, as I said, it brought to mind that Henri also disappeared about the same time and right after *Mouth of Steel* was published, which is very very interesting indeed because the novel is a *roman à clef* insofar as the main character is concerned, who is based on Annette Lorpailleur, who was tied up with Pungoe in Christ knows what

kind of eerie, eerie whatever. What I'm getting at is that Henri and
Annette didn't get on too well, as a matter of fact he used to call her
Mademoiselle Mummy because she stood so stiff and still and because
of that voice, that *voice* of hers that didn't really quite come out of her.
She'd talk and her mouth would move but it was as if the whole thing
was from an out-of-synch movie, the mouth was moving but, you
know, either just in front of or just behind, I mean just before and after
what she was saying, I used to think it was almost inhuman, for Christ
sake. In any event, Hicks disappeared, then Henri disappeared. And
dear Jack got caught up in this building con and, well, you know what
happened.

Can you give me a brief synopsis of *La Bouche métallique* or
Mouth of Steel?

Oh sure, though it's been a long time since I've read it, not since
it first came out, really, though I was looking through it, oddly enough,
just a couple of weeks ago. You have to understand that it's not really
representative, as they say, of Henri's best work, his poems, and he
wrote some really terrific prose poems too, they're really his best
work. *Mouth of Steel* was written as a kind of lurid melodrama, sinister and strange, I think that Henri, in his ignorance, thought that
maybe it would make him some money, maybe the movies would pick
it up or somebody would take an option on it, lots of luck, that was
strictly a pipe dream. The book is much too complicated, too convoluted for the geniuses of the cinema to do anything with it, even
though it's got a lot of intentional soap opera in it. All right, I'm going
by memory and all I can do is give you the barest essentials. First of
all, the book is in three parts, each one a different kind of part, I mean
different stories, sort of, different characters. There are three main
characters in the first part, a guy named Dick Grande, another, Jack
Rube, and a woman whose name is given only as Madame Jeannette,
who is in the finest tradition of the beat-me-please genre, a stern,
harsh, disciplinarian, what do they call that in the porno-flick ads, a
dominatrix? I think so, not quite the hip boots black stockings and
whips routine but quite clearly the same type. O.K., there you have the

main three. We find out that Jack Rube has fallen under the spell of Madame Jeannette, so much so that he ignores and mistreats his wife who loves him dearly, and so on and so forth, and his career, whatever the hell he is, or does, some noble lawyer or brilliant academic, his career is suffering because he sits around all day dreaming of crawling on his hands and knees in front of Madame J, begging her to humiliate him, force him to write bad checks and wear thin white socks, I'm kidding, but yes, he does get off on being used. So, enter Dick Grande, old pal called by Jack's wife, they all went to college together, he's now a marine biologist or a cave explorer, some dumb kind of TV gig, and of course we discover that he used to love Jack's wife when they all went to Suntan U, but he lost the girl, you've been here before of course, at least a thousand times. In steps stalwart Dick to rescue his old fraternity buddy from his obsession. By now, Jack is kicking the cat, leaving the house without his plaid sport coat, throwing his wife's tuna-avocado casseroles on the floor and insulting her Peck and Peck blouses and her sensible shoes, I mean the *works*. But what happens is that Dick goes to see Madame Jeannette in her penthouse, what else? She enchants him, oh, I forgot to tell you, this is central to the book, the title and everything else, the Madame has a mouth made out of *steel*, right. And there are very strong hints and then a fairly explicit scene dealing with Madame's steel mouth and her erotic use of it, she's just a good-time girl who can do all sorts of tricks with the old *bouche*, make you jump for joy. In a flash *Dick* becomes her sex slave and is enraged that he has to share his delicious degradation with his pal, Jack, so with the help of Madame Jeannette and, unwittingly, Jack's sweet, intelligent, charming, witty, and deeply loving and caring and nurturing wife, he destroys Jack's career and his life and Jack winds up a wreck condemned to live out his days in Scranton or someplace, a shopping mall, a mere shell of a man. End of first part. Second part. The story is told over again, this time changed around a little, a strong and imperious woman, Jeannette, who is not averse to giving her beloved husband a few vigorous lashes regular as clockwork, her husband being Dick Grande, meets a handsome and rather vague professor of something or other, who is one Jack Rube, only now he's called Dr. John Rube, and despite his degrees, his Phi Beta Kappa key, his tweed pipes and briar jackets, his vacations in Europe and his near-adoration of Yvor Winters, he succumbs to his powerful yet till now repressed desire, his desperate need, to grovel, crawl, lick high-heeled shoes, be beaten and laced into tight corsets, and so on and so forth, tendencies no doubt developed during all the years he waited to get tenure. Jeannette, with the aid of a metal face mask that she fastens on Jack when he's been especially good, it's his reward for especially fine writhing and begging, Jeannette persuades him to kill her old man for his big insurance bread, dumb old Dick, who can't understand why his old lady only canes him once a week lately, he's beginning to think the honeymoon is over. So Dick is dispatched by Dr. Rube, who drowns him in the bathtub or the toilet, then rushes wildly to the arms of Jeannette, or I should say crawls to the legs of Jeannette, whimpering for his metal face mask and a few kicks. But! entering her bedroom he sees that Jeannette is a *man*! Yes, this powerful, brawny, imposing, and strapping woman is not a woman at all but a powerful, brawny and so forth man! But the good doctor doesn't mind, he's too enamored to let a little thing like gender stand in the way of happiness. Jeannette is not pleased, however, and she puts the mask on him in such a way that he suffocates, and she arranges the whole thing to make it look like a bizarre homosexual murder-suicide. That's part two. The third part is in the form of a notebook, a journal, whatever, in the first person, that's being kept by a nun, Sister Jeannette, the story in the journal being that of a woman that she knew, named, coincidentally, Jeannette, a sincere, devout, chaste woman who has been totally corrupted by two men, Jack and Dick, successful and in the eyes of the world, of course, wonderful, first-rate gents, but who are in reality two vicious sadists who hate women and spend their lives and wealth corrupting the innocent and good. The twist is that one of these guys enjoys his secret-life adventures dressed as a nun, in this way he gains the confidence of modest women and so on and so forth. However, we discover as we read that the journal tells a shad-

owy story of murder and blackmail stemming from some compromising photographs of the so-called nun, I mean the guy who dresses like
a nun, photographs with a priest who, it turns out, has also had something going with Jeannette, whom we thought was chaste, devout, and
so on. Just as the book reaches this point we come upon a new entry
that reads, more or less—That's the novel I'd like to write if I had the
time and the talent. So we know that Sister Jeannette has written this.
O.K., now things shift again, the view is objective, third person, we see
Sister Jeannette undressing, we get loving and meticulous details of
her movements and garments, and then we find that Sister Jeannette
is a man just like the wife in the second part, *then* we see her, or I
should say him dressing like a priest, as you can see things are getting
more lurid by the minute, and now it gets very weird. The priest puts
his nun's clothes on a mannequin made out of polished steel that's
standing in the corner, then he pushes a button and the mannequin
starts to speak. There's a tape recorder or whatever in the mannequin's head and the damn thing starts to talk and what it says is the
first part, verbatim, of *Mouth of Steel*! After a paragraph or two, given
absolutely word for word, the priest switches off the machine or re-
winds it, whatever, and he then starts to dictate into the mannequin's
mouth—and what he dictates are the opening sentences of the *second*
part of *this* book, I mean *Mouth of Steel*. And the book ends. That's it,
with an awful lot of details and odds and ends and minor characters
left out. It's an odd item. It was almost completely ignored and the
language is weird because of the disastrous double translation, so to
speak. But you can still find an odd copy at pretty steep prices since
it's become a kind of cult classic.

     Tell me some more about Annette Lorpailleur—for instance,
what did she do at this party?

     Well, I don't know too much about her because as I've said al-
ready, she was mysterious and involved in things that I didn't really
want to know about, and still don't for that matter, but she *was* beautiful. A big woman, about thirty-five, must have stood six feet tall in
her stocking feet, beautiful body, jet-black hair, and these strange

pale-blue, ice-blue eyes that never seemed quite in focus, but still, it's hard to explain, still seemed as if they were looking right into your brain. She just *appeared* one day and started to pop up at parties, openings, a supposed partner, as I've told you, with Harlan Pungoe in some sort of business dealings. Then it was thought that she was a kind of patron of Annie Flammard after Annie took a powder from Canada, Annie hinted, in fact, that she'd known her in Canada, but I always thought that she was from somewhere in Europe, France or Switzerland. Anyway, that's not important, except that Bart Kahane told me that Conchita, his ex, as you remember, that she wrote him from Paris that she'd met some very strange woman there at a book party by the name of Roberte Flambeaux, and her description was a perfect one of Annette, which leads us right into the soup because Roberte Flambeaux was, right? supposedly Annie Flammard's real name, although it's often struck me that this rumor about Annie's so-called real name was very carefully put out by Annie herself as a smokescreen, a blind, I mean, she's the source, as if she wanted to divert attention from Annette. Annette gave Annie a kind of allowance to live on so she could paint and, wait a minute. No, she was making sculpture then and Annette sometimes would buy pieces from her as well, paid very nice prices, even though Annie had no gallery, no dealer, and no real reputation at all. One piece I especially remember, a big piece, polished steel, aluminum, chrome and nickel, called *Gin City*, that Annette had right in the middle of the living-room floor. And there was another one, smaller, but still a big piece, up on a wall, sort of a wall piece, that's a brilliant observation, and that was copper or bronze, polished like a mirror. That one was later sold by Annette, I think, I can't remember the name of it, it was either *Steel Orange*, after Cecil's book, it was a kind of rough globe in shape, right, or it was called *99*, don't ask me why, I can't recall. They never struck me as very good pieces. The assumption was that Annette and Annie were, you know, getting it on together, to tell you the truth all the men were envious of Annie except that you always had the feeling that hopping into bed with Madame Lorpailleur would be like screwing a robot or maybe a refrigerator. Anyway these pieces did, I suppose, complement the apartment, this was when Annette was living in this opulent co-op with Corrie Corriendo and Madame Delamode. These were two hookers who had been around, *professionals*, still-attractive women who'd had some sort of spectacular porno racket going somewhere, Mexico City, I think. I understand that they published porno magazines and made films that featured middle-aged, matronly looking women and hit a huge, untapped market. Just when you think you've heard it all, right? And they also ran some porno distribution service on the side, made a *lot* of money and then left and came here. They were supposed to have some sort of sensational magic act in a club that they owned themselves, some little trap, I think it was called The Blue Ruin, long closed now. I caught part of their act once, they were good, but the real attraction was that they were only half-dressed if that on stage, a lot of bare flesh, you know, and they had a shill or two in the audience at the show I saw, the last show, good-looking young women, built, you know, and they ran this game down about the power of suggestion and these women got up as if they were hypnotized, sure they were, and mechanically stripped down to their panties before a couple of waiters rushed up to cover them, you know, to the rescue! Believe me, the customers ate it up, and everything I heard about the place proved that it just got more and more popular, you couldn't get in the damn place even on a weekday night. What was I saying? Oh yes, they were all three living together in this apartment and it was incredible, did I tell you about it? I don't think so, but it's worth telling. The place was all *metal*. Absolutely, the whole goddam place, steel and copper and bronze, I mean literally *made* out of metal, the walls, the ceilings, the floors, all the fixtures and the tubs and the toilets, the refrigerators, bookcases, I mean *everything*. Even the mirrors were some kind of polished metal, aluminum I think. There was one room that I went into by mistake one night at a dinner party that they gave for something, I think it was the opening of Barnett's little boutique, the Soirée Intime, I told you about it, in which they maybe had some sort of financial interest, the place was strictly a terminal for Tete's dirty money, a little laundry to wash it all white, you know? And it wouldn't surprise me if Annette and Pungoe got in on this to stash some of their loot from the mail-order cult scam, or the other scams they probably had going. Anyway, this room I went into was all red metal, this blood-red copper or some damn thing, and all over the walls were these weird hieroglyphics, scribbles, whatever, and a little, it looked like a little altar in the corner, there were no windows in the room and it must have been below freezing in there, I was in and out in a flash, there was something strange going down there, I mean this was not the family room with Old Shep dozing in the corner and the roaring blaze. This was heavyweight bizarre. The dinner party was more or less O.K., I've been to worse, amen. The strange thing was that Annette and Corrie and Madame were dressed in matching black gowns that were made of *metal*, and they had on, this was really something, metal shoes and stockings! I don't mean *metallic*, that glittery fabric, I mean *metal* in thin, thin sheets, or maybe the things were made out of metal thread, something, but the McCoy, Jesus, they almost clanked when they moved. You can imagine this, the place itself, their clothes, and so on, in tandem with Annette and that voice of hers. And the other two who talked with these absurd accents, as I've mentioned, these accents that sounded as if they came out of a movie, you didn't know whether they were supposed to be Italian or French or Mexican or lower Bulgarian for that matter. But if you heard them talk when they didn't mean for you to hear them, they sounded like they were Whytte-Blorenge's sisters, dese dose and dems—for all I know they may well have been, they came out of oblivion, and, wait a minute. I just thought of something about them, Léonie told me this, she happened to be there once with Tete, their affair was dying at the time since Luba, or I should say Sylvie was already on the scene, though I really don't remember if Tete had given her this new name yet, it's not important. Good old Barnett was surely sleeping with both of them with Léonie already second banana, but whatever the case Sylvie wasn't at this party that Annette and the Dolly Sisters gave. Léonie said that there was some guy there all dressed up like an officer in some foreign army, French or Italian or something, braids and medals and ribbons and stars and Christ knows what else, strictly comic opera, the works, a big tall guy who was soaking up the booze and talking about books and art and music, the whole deeply cultured and cosmopolitan front, right? like a nightmare that you're in San Francisco and you'll never be able to leave. And as he's doing all this talking he's giving a little feel here and a little squeeze there to all the women, very subtle, with this Charles Boyer voice. I can't remember the women who were there but he was hitting on all of them, the major part of his line had to do with a novel he'd just read in London, ahem, called, I think, *The Orange Dress* by somebody named Thelma something, some kind of a Polish name, Krulewicz or Krelewicz, Krulicewicz maybe, and coming on about how it was all about him and his family, the author had worked as a secretary for his father who was some kind of a big-time diplomat or some damn thing. The kind of lame shit that you can hear at any party but he had it all down pat, smooth and sweet, with his bedroom eyes and continental manner, the headwaiter routine in spades. Anyway, to make a long story short, to tell you a little more about the, about Annette and company, which is what the point of this digression is all about, anyway, he disappeared a couple of times with, and I'm only telling you what Léonie told me, a couple of different women, Sheila Henry and April, which you can almost make a mean joke out of in a way. I mean I can imagine Lou saying, Hey baby, go ahead, maybe we can like buy the original manuscript of *The Orange Dress*, give the frog a little poon, you'll never miss it, and April, well. Dick would be like under the bed or in the shower stall with his Rolex and light meters and whatever the fuck else, whispering Look abandoned, baby! Stick your tongue out! Roll your eyes! All right, maybe that's unfair. Anyway. The point of all this is that as the party was breaking up, Annette introduces this officer of the imperial household and horse dragoons or hussars or whatever he was supposed to be as some deadbeat actor she hired for the occasion and this guy, some Oaky Doaks, takes a bow and thanks everyone for such a wonderful time. April and Sheila are minutely scrutinizing their nails, right? O.K. That gives you a little more of an idea of these three women, especially the boss, Annette, just a barrel of laughs. And Léonie added that she also heard later that every room in the apartment had hidden tape recorders and movie cameras, so there might well still be some *remarkable* pictures floating around of various citizens, you know, the kind of things that might give the relatives back on the farm something to think about at Christmas. Noël, Noël. That's really all I can tell you, generally speaking, about Annette—you did want to know about *her*, right? The Platinum Priestess as Jack Towne called her, God it's long ago. So that's, oh, of course, your question. I imagine you mean Horace's party for Bart? It's hard to say because she was with her little clique, they weren't concerned with the goings on of Leo and his two wives and Marowitz poking you in the chest with his fat finger and spitting potato salad all over your tie, you remember that fiasco. She was with *her* people, dear Pungoe, the Flem Snopes of our time, you can throw Popeye in too, and Roger the shoe lover, who else? Oh yes, Lorna Flambeaux who had something going at that time with Guy, he took her to Horace's that night as I recall. So. I can't tell you what she did, there was just that eerie, that uncanny *thing* about her, that power she had—I know it sounds ridiculous— that power over people. I do remember her asking Guy about Lucy Taylor, plain Jane, who was, I think, living with Lou and Sheila at the time, though that may have been later, she was asking him about Lucy's amour with Bunny, only, well, only at that particular time *nobody* knew about it, Guy and Bunny were still going through the motions, Guy even denied the whole thing to himself, as they say. But Annette was talking about this as if it had been on the front page, you know what I mean? Oh yes, there was also something that Lena told me she overheard standing outside the bathroom. She heard people talking and realized it was Annette, nobody could mistake that voice, *no body*, and some guy, so Lena figured that Annette was having a little quick romance on the tiles, but then five minutes later she realizes that they're *just* talking, serious talk, not the wingèd words of love. What she gets, in bits and pieces, is Annette talking about some hotel or rooming house that has something to do with Barnett or Pungoe or maybe the both of them, but she got the impression that the place was going to be or maybe already had been torched. Some place called the Lincoln Inn or the Lincstone? I can't recall. O.K., the door opens and Lena makes some lame joke about her teeth floating or says Aha! love in bloom, to cover herself. The guy is none other than Joizy Cidy Rog, the old heels humper, Thom McAn in person. Lena said that Annette gave her a look that would have stopped a tank in its tracks. That's it as far as I know about Annette at that party. But a fleabag called the Lincoln Inn or whatever it was did burn down about a week after that and six people were killed.

What did April Detective see when she entered Mr. Rosette's study?

April wasn't at the party for Bart as far as I know, though I don't really know, maybe she came late, I don't think so. But I'm sure she *entered*, as you put it, Horace's study many times. As I've said, Horace was always giving a party or having some sort of get-together for drinks after an opening or a show or when the bars closed, he was a good-time Charlie with a slight weakness for the genitals of warm bodies, a mere peccadillo. I remember when he first met Lena, she almost turned him into the complete heterosexual because, my God, her little limp got him all hot and bothered, he'd have done anything to get her into bed, he went on and on about flawed beauty and tainted perfection, sounded like a bush-league Gabriel Rossetti. Lena took it all in stride, she had, as they say, a lot of class, lovely girl, and Christ knows she was *very* good-looking, Jack Towne heard about it and gave Horace a little tap or two and told him to lay off Lena and get his fag scene in gear again, if you'll pardon the expression, the way Jack put it he said, Go with your strength. Anyway Horace had a perpetual soirée of sorts, you were liable to meet anyone at his place any time, thus, so to speak, April. Vague yet sweet, maybe too sweet. Maybe you could say rotten. There was that air of corruption about her, although that simply might have been later when she and Dick started in on their dirty-picture obsession. I mean maybe she was the girl in the pink dress and Dick twisted her around, I don't know. As I say, anyway, April could have and did enter Horace's study, I'm sure, many a time, and as to what she saw there, well. You were liable to see *anything* in Horace's study, it was more or less understood that it was strictly open city, proceed at your own risk, you know? I can tell you about one time that I know about because I was there with Tania, she and I were then intimate, as they say, this was before she was the chic manager of Barnett's chic shop, still a human being, you could still talk to her, she was as a matter of fact a lot of fun. We were seeing a hell of a lot of each other. We were even thinking of getting married. Just as well I guess, she had her eye on the dollar and her nose in the air even then but when she took her clothes off all was forgiven, amen. She was really something special. So the night I know about, or the day, whatever, this was really long ago, years ago, as I said, Dick had just bought his first camera and hadn't yet started to stick his goddam light meters in your face, I remember it completely because it was the first time that I was really aware of what a weird bitch Annette was. I should tell you that at this time, let me see, Jack Towne was not only alive but, you know, clean, he hadn't got into the dirty-money scene yet, so it was maybe twenty years ago, anyway, Lou Henry and April were having a very discreet affair just about that time, I think that only a few people knew about it, one of those things, as they say, that just happened. I knew about it because April told Tania, they were friends then, maybe they still are for all I know, but not the way they were, April later on worked for Tania when she managed Soirée Intime, she used to model the lingerie for the annual catalogue they put out, they charged ten bucks a copy for it unless you had an account at the store, quite a little item, a discreet aid, so to speak, to sexuality, or, to be crass, a classic jerk-off magazine in the guise of a catalogue, well, that was later. I knew about Lou and April because of Tania, it was accidental the way it started, par for the course, right? Lou and Sheila were already involved in a very minor way with Saul and the manuscript collecting, I guess they'd just started, certainly the first thing they bought was the manuscript and notes and such of a book called, if I remember rightly, *Blackjack*, by Christ knows who, he never wrote another book, whoever it was, or never published anyway, his name's on the tip of my tongue, Richard, Pritchard? Hell, I don't remember. Anyway, they bought this stuff, the book was never published. It might have been, as a matter of fact, the very first thing they bought, their entree into the fabled world of collecting, now you too can know the thrill. In any event, some schmuck made a fifteen-minute movie out of the book, you know, hand-held cameras, cinema vérité business, filmed on the teeming ever-changing streets with no decent lighting. It was shown as part of a program, one of those midnight-to-dawn programs they used to run in arty fleabag theaters, every son of a bitch who ever owned a cheap camera came and stayed the whole night for a buck and a half. Well, Lou went to see what had been done to his *property*, very proprietary, right? And who should be there but Mrs. Dick Detective, who had been asked by the esteemed poet and editor, Craig Garf, to write a review of one of the films, maybe *Blackjack*, for all I know, for *Lorzu*, the little magazine I mentioned that he was using as his flying carpet to what the poor ridiculous bastard thought of as success, Jesus Christ! Now April could write a decent letter as they say, she could spell, you know, but as a writer, forget it, so why Craig asked her to do this, your guess is as good as mine. I don't think that anything so obvious would get April out of her dress but who knows? In less than a year she was up to her eyes with the old man in kinky pictures and whatever else, the whole scene, so maybe Craig had some inkling of this or saw, as they say, into her true nature, her true self, if you'll pardon the phrase. Well, this is all by the way, the story is that they bumped into each other at this theater and talked, left after a while and had some coffee and one thing as it will led to another and they went to bed in, I think, Lucy Taylor's apartment, Lucy was discreet and so on and besides she had no love for either Dick or Sheila. The point of all this is that they really fell for each other and it got very sticky indeed. April and Dick were already living in Connecticut and for her to see Lou was a production, she had to beg Craig Garf to carry her as the film critic on the *Lorzu* masthead, so that way she could get into town maybe once every two weeks to see some film, sure, on the ceiling, right? Tania knew all about this by now, so when April came into town she let her stay at her place and Lou would come over and spend the night, what story he gave Sheila Christ only knows, but that's the way it went. O.K. Now the Rosette business, right, that was really a kind of touch of, what can I call it? monstrosity, perversity. Whatever the occasion or absence of occasion, Horace's place was jammed and his study was, as usual, in *use*, if you follow me, and Annette Lorpailleur got hold of April and told her that she was really interested in talking to her about having her and Dick spend a weekend with her and meet some of her friends, a wonderful painter and her wonderful friend, who else? Annie Flammard and Barry Gatto, the Gold Dust Twins. Annie was also a *brilliant* photographer, oh yes indeed, and Annette had heard that Dick was looking for a good teacher, a private teacher, and so on and so forth, how *lucky*, how *marvelous* for all of us. That voice coming out of the chandelier or the wall. And I've really wanted so much to get to *know* you better, Annette says. I've heard *so much* about you and your husband. You mustn't be strangers and exile yourselves in the country. Even though the country is so wonderful, so peaceful. I was brought up in the country, she says, right, the work farm no doubt, and on and on, and April, who was a simple soul, is listening to all this shit. Then Annette says to her that they might go into Horace's study, so nice and quiet, a few people listening to Vivaldi and blowing a little boss weed, away from the madding crowd, so they go in. Well, it was, to coin a phrase, gangbusters indeed indeed, I heard the story later, I don't recall who told me, not important anyway. The room was dim, maybe one or two soft lamps on, and under one of them there were clothes, a pile of clothes, slips, bras, men's things, all sorts of things, and as April starts to realize what she's seeing she notes, notes is good, she notes the real center of attraction, the center ring, so to speak, and lo! it's the Henrys, Lou and Sheila, and not to go into obscene detail but they're both on their knees with Lou giving it to Sheila from behind, I mean he's, you know, and both of them drunk or stoned and Sheila is crazy, Sheila is, Sheila's going down on Bunny, and in a chair watching this whole thing is that good ole boy, Harlan P, his honest hands calloused and worn from hauling himself up by his own bootstraps, and he's taking pictures, a true American, true and fucking blue American, presidential caliber. What Annette was up to Christ only knows but as far as I'm concerned she had le hot for April and figured she'd just try her luck, the element of surprise, who knows? April might have been turned on except that she and Lou, well, she almost collapsed right there, Lou looked up for a second and just smiled, didn't miss a beat, Sheila was too busy to look at anything, Bunny tried to hide her face but there she was in all her naked glory, with Harlan slobbering away and panting and grunting and making noises, and going click click click with his trusty Kodak. Anyway, Bunny, Bunny in the middle of the scene was proof, if anybody needed any proof, that she was still at that time paying off for Guy's, shall we say, association? with Harlan's direct-mail con, paying off Harlan, I mean. There's no mystery why she and Lucy became lovers, not at all, every time she turned around some guy was taking her over the hurdles in one way or another, Pungoe, of course, was the greatest bastard of them all. He always had plenty of allies, so to speak, but he especially walked on Bunny as if she were a rug, she was *used* by him, what's the word I'm looking for? Soiled, right, she was *soiled* by him. It had been going on for years and years, ever since Bunny was a girl, really. He had her by the short hairs, had a lot of pictures of her that he'd set up, some phony poses and plenty that were not so phony, she was into smack when she was young and Harlan was her connection, he'd hold out on her till she'd do what he wanted, when she finally got straight she got out from under him and then she met Guy. Out of the blue comes Pungoe, surprise surprise! How nice to see you again, Miss Ward, Ward was Bunny's maiden name, oh? you're Mrs. Lewis now? How nice! Maybe we can have lunch or a drink sometime.

Do I understand you to mean that Joanne Lewis—Bunny—had know Harlan Pungoe long before she met Guy?

Oh hell, yes. I thought I made that clear, I'm sorry. It's all in the dim past, as Doctor Plot might write, as a matter of fact, he probably

has, a few hundred times. Bunny dropped out of college after some
sort of a disastrous affair with some guy whose family had come over
on the *Mayflower*, probably in a little boat a few hundred yards in front
of the thing, and when they found out that their very own Myles Stan-
dish was serious about this common type who had no breeding, no
background, no cash, they stepped in and broke it up. Bunny took it
very hard. She started to hit the sauce pretty good, then split, and as
the story went, she wound up in the vast beyond somewhere, Nevada
or Montana, New Mexico, where men are men and sunglasses are
king. She was about twenty, you understand, maybe only nineteen, this
was almost twenty years ago, eighteen anyway, and she got a job in
some hip little bar as a cocktail waitress or barmaid or something,
getting her ass pinched, etcetera. O.K. Who should be working in the
joint but a guy named Baylor Freeq, who was really Biff Page sailing
under false colors because he was on the run, nothing really serious,
he'd been hanging paper here and there, had this Western manly con
going, Stetson, boots, jeans, he'd just charm the hell out of some poor
gullible rube bastard talking about the goddam New York Jews and
commies and how Jesus was good enough for him and passing his bad
checks right and left. Where he got the name Baylor Freeq Christ only
knows, the funny thing is that his father had plenty of money, Biff was
the black sheep or some damn thing, didn't want to go into the business. The usual old tale. Anyway, he and Bunny went out together a
few times, had a few laughs, then one day some humble citizen shows
up, Biff introduces Bunny to him, who else but our friend Harlan? He's
very considerate, sweet, mature, a marriage gone sour because of an
alcoholic wife, hat in hand, digs his toe into the floor, the old Gary
Cooper con, just a hard-working fella, true blue, and despite his club
foot a salesman who through snow and hail and so on, the sorta kinda
guy, the kinda *little* guy that's made America what it is. Any fucking
cliché you can think of, that's Harlan. He also happened to know that
a little taste of heroin now and again couldn't hurt a fly, well, not to
give you a scenario, good ole Harlan turned Bunny on, her understanding soulmate, they got high together, the old boring story once

again, and one fine morning what do you know? Bunny has this very persistent ugly Jones, absolutely addicted. So Harlan said, well my dear girl, of course you can have what you need but first let's have some good clean honest fun. Fun to Harlan was not only the voyeur scene, Bunny with Biff, Bunny with some hookers he hired, Bunny with a couple of truck drivers, Bunny with anything and everything, plus of course Harlan's camera in action, it was also making Bunny beat him, whip him, and vice versa, a whole sadomasochist scene, boots and saddles. This went on for maybe two years, maybe more, a love story played out against the breathtaking panorama of the fabled West. As I say, this went on and on, Bunny was a zombie, when she wasn't full of smack she was soaking up the booze, and at least once a week she'd be the star of one of Harlan's parties. In between times she and her benefactor would stage their own little scenes, Bunny told me once that Harlan's favorite was the little play where he'd surprise her in the bathroom and then beg to be punished for being so dirty, so lewd and so foul, then after she beat him he'd beat her for daring to beat him. A twisted son of a bitch. But once in a while Harlan would have to leave on business, selling, as he said. The selling turned out to be some arrangement he had in Mexico, his porno pictures would bring him some good money, of course, beautiful co-ed in shameless acts of lust, and so on, then he'd buy some good Mexican grass and get it across the border, sell that and buy up, buy some skag, and so on and so forth, he had his connections all over the place, a knight of the trackless sands. He'd leave Biff a maintenance ration of shit for Bunny and off he'd go. Well I don't really know how it happened but I do know Biff was involved, a fit of remorse or something, but she managed to cold turkey once when Harlan was gone for two weeks, Biff sold the dope and gave her the money and she ran for her life. There may have been many more complications to the story, I don't know, I heard this a long time after, some of it from Bunny, some from Guy, and some from Chico Zeek, but to be fair, I also heard from Sylvie that Pungoe hadn't been involved at all, that, as a matter of fact, Harlan had never met Bunny before he came to town. But that doesn't make much sense because then I can't figure out why Bunny would allow herself to be involved in such things as the scene in Horace's study, and I understand, hell, I *know*, that Bunny was involved in a number of scenes like that, all presided over, if you will, by Harlan. I mean I can't understand it if Harlan didn't have something on her, I mean those photographs, right? Anyway, that's none of my business. But then, what is? Bunny met Guy at some picnic or something given by Lincoln, Save the rats! or some damn thing, I seem to remember that he managed, Lincoln I mean, he managed some nature bookshop at the time, Black Ladder Books I think, a hell of a name. Well, she and Guy hit it off, they started living together, and I guess eventually got sort of married. Guy got a job as day bartender at a little joint that was a hang-out for artists, Caliph's Walk. It had been, of all things, a Chinese restaurant originally, by Omaha a Chinese restaurant, a dump called the Red Silk, I think, strictly chop suey and fortune cookies, a big drunk business after the bars closed. Anyway, Bunny came to some sort of understanding with her parents and they gave her a small allowance so she could go back to school. Nice, normal life, you know? Enter Pungoe. The great rube appeared, as I've said, out of nowhere, I don't remember how or even exactly when, but I can swear it wasn't because of Biff Page because when Harlan appeared Biff wasn't in town, he'd gone on a buying trip for his father, his wild oats sowed, whatever, he wasn't around anyway. Harlan had what he called this great-potential mail-order business in the works and he started to talk about it to people, and as it turned out, one of the people he talked to was Guy, because Harlan used to have lunch every day at the Caliph's Walk bar. And whether Sylvie was right or not, somehow Harlan made it clear to Guy that he could get in on this scam, big bucks a-comin'! and opportunity unlimited and so on, he made it clear to Guy that he'd have to meet the little woman. The plot thickens. So Guy, ignorant of everything, Sylvie *had* to be wrong, it's clearer and clearer, Guy, ignorant of everything and excited about the job, tells Bunny. She hears the name but what can she say? I used to be involved in orgies with Harlan and friends? I heard that they had dinner, Tania told me, and Bunny

laughed, chatted, was vivacious and charming and so on, acted absolutely dumb, well of course in Harlan's sweaty pocket he probably
had some interesting pictures, to say the least, of the fresh and vibrant
Mrs. Lewis with two truck drivers and a slut out of some rundown
cathouse, all in living color. If you put two and two together it must
have turned out that for Guy to get the job *and* remain ignorant of the
pictures, Bunny had to have a party or two with Pungoe, poor unfortunate man probably hadn't been whipped in months. Love will find
a way. So miracle of miracles! The job came through for Guy, he quit
bartending and started to work for Harlan. Thought it was his charm
and intelligence that got him the job. The odd thing about it all was
that when Harlan came on the scene, nobody really thought that he
was an A number one bastard, I have to be honest about it and say that
I didn't either. Oh yeah, he was strictly a rube, at least that was his act,
his unbelievable suits, Jesus, he had one that was, he called it electric
blue, enough to send you screaming into the night, and ties! Oh my
God, you know those insanely hideous hand-painted ties they used to
sell? That's all Harlan owned, burn the eyes right out of your head. But
as far as being, well, sinister, no, I didn't think so. Some people even
thought that he was a great guy, you know, a lot of ole boy stories,
working on the farm, his days as a labor organizer, travels all over the
world, merchant seaman, the works, right? Man of the people, the soil,
he played to that vague romantic crap about rural folk, I guess we
were all taken in by him. Correction, not *all*. April, this was just before
she married Dick, she hated the man. She'd never say why but she did,
she and Dick had a lot of quarrels about it I heard, as a matter of fact,
I myself heard a lot of the quarrels. Dick thought Harlan was aces, ole
Pungoe would set the bar up, tell his hick stories and on and on, bump
around on his fucking club foot, but April would, I can't explain it,
she'd literally get rigid with anger, *fury*, whenever she saw him, I
don't think a word ever passed between them. Harlan *had* to know
how she felt so it must have been a great night for him when Annette
took her into Horace's study and there was Lou in the middle of it.
Jesus, now that I think about it, it's odd how these things come clear,

now that I think of it, Harlan must have known all about Lou and April and that's why he arranged with Annette for April to be taken into the study. Oh Christ, of course. He gave her, as they say, an eyeful, had the last laugh.

But if what you've said about April Detective is true, how do you explain these photographs of her?

Photographs of her? Let's see. If I may. I'll be damned. I don't have any idea unless, wait a minute. These must have been taken some time later, I mean long after April and Dick split up. Maybe April and Harlan became friends, though that's very unlikely, or else it was just one of those things since Sylvie is in, what? three of these shots and April and Sylvie got to know each other very well about the time that Dick started to carry on with Karen Ostrom, she must have charmed him with some magical wheat germ. What's funny to me is that this looks like, I mean this obviously is an adobe house, so I guess Harlan must have left his heart, and a bank account, in the far-flung Southwest. Unless April and Harlan, no, I doubt that, I was going to say that maybe April's dislike for Harlan was just so much eyewash. I suppose that's possible but I can't figure out why she'd go to all the trouble of making it *look* as if she loathed the man. I really don't know. My best guess is, as I say, that Sylvie, as a friend, asked April to take a vacation from Dick and his behavior with Karen, Vance was dead by this time, I don't remember if I told you that? Well, it's not important, but yes, he was dead then, he died in a fire in one of those phony country inns in New England, The Red Swan, phony name, phony sign, I wouldn't be at all surprised if it said, you know, Ye Olde Redde Swanne Inne, one of those dodges, some city slicker probably opened the joint to con the Sunday drivers out to look at the autumn leaves. Anyway, the place burned down, Vance was trapped in his bathroom, what the hell he was doing there I don't know, but they found him the next day dead of smoke inhalation. I found out later that he was dressed like a woman, he was wearing a white silk dress, panties, nylons, high heels, everything. It was quite a shock because nobody ever figured that Vance was kinky. Somebody suggested that the whole thing was hushed up, and it pretty much was, because it looked as if there was some sort of funny business going on up there, it was a common rumor that Jack Marowitz owned this joint, I mean, he was behind it, you know, it was some sort of corporation, but I don't believe that, Jack had had his fill of the real-estate business years before with Lincoln, so I doubt if he'd have been involved. The whole thing just sort of died, they held an inquest, I think, but nothing came of it, but nobody has yet explained what Vance was doing in drag in this cutesy New England inn. Anyway, I'm getting off the track here. You know, I don't want to be difficult or rude, not at all, but I don't know what it is you're getting at with these questions. It would probably be better for you to talk to somebody who has access to, you know, real information, I mean hard data, as they say. I certainly *knew* these people but I was, as the phrase goes, leading my own life during all this time. I had things to do, jobs, I was married for a while, and these people kept moving around, doing this and that, I don't know much more than what I saw, not a hell of a lot, and what I heard, which is always colored, you know how people do that. I mean you could ask questions forever and just, well, just produce more questions. I don't mind, you understand, but I'm human. I mean to say I can forget things or just get them wrong. All right. In any event, let me see if I can put things together to explain these photographs. I don't mean explain them, I mean see if I can somehow cogently, right, cogently, if I can offer a cogent reason, rather, for these photographs. As I've told you, April and Sylvie became really good friends after Vance died, not that he had anything to do with them but Dick then had a clear field with Karen, well, you know this, anyway, they were good friends and were collaborating on a book, one of those fast-buck deals, how to dress rich with, you know, the best little stores listed, places to buy chic but inexpensive clothes, how to have *real* style, the kind of dumb thing that would go over big with the faithful hip who read *Hip Vox*, as a matter of fact, Lee Jefferson had given them the idea, as I recall. She'd arranged with them to have lunch with her and some acquisitions editor, how I love that phrase, some lover of literature complete with faded jeans and the right politics whose name, thanks be to Christ, escapes me. The thing fell through because of Barnett, who didn't want Sylvie doing anything that might have enabled her to get out from under the boutique, his first boutique, not the Soirée Intime. Barnett liked to keep his women on a maintenance diet, *just* enough but always there if they were good little girls, Sylvie, Léonie, and Tania, only Tania finally escaped, more or less, because the Soirée Intime got so much breathless ink that she became a kind of media celebrity, titillating articles about transparent bras and such, the outrageous prices they charged, the famous catalogue, the stories about staid businessmen coming in for underwear for themselves, all that rubbish. Interviews, talk shows, oh and she was *terrific.* The lowered eyes, the slight blush, the demurely crossed legs with her skirt pulled just so over her knees, in the meantime she's talking to some slobbering host about women's freedom and crotchless panties. Sometimes I can't really believe that we were actually married, *briefly*, but it's as if it happened to somebody else. Anyway. The photographs, right, April and Harlan smiling into the sun, O.K. All I can guess is that Harlan had nothing to do with it, so to speak, I mean really nothing at all, because it was probably a case of Sylvie asking April to take a short vacation at what must have been, maybe not, Harlan's house wherever the hell it was and Harlan was there when they arrived or he showed up. I just don't know. I'll tell you one thing that intrigues me though and that's who *took* these shots of the three of them together. Did they recruit some passing Indian or a lonesome cowboy? Not that it matters, but I'd just like to know. It's possible, just barely, that it was Dick, he and April *might* have gone together, singing that old sweet song, let's-try-it-one-more-time to the silv'ry moon and the desert breezes. But if it was Dick you can bet your ass that it was because Miss Whole-Grains had to go home, all smiles, freckles, and gleaming teeth, to see the old folks in Apple Pie, Nebraska. He and Harlan could have had long talks in front of the cheery blaze about lenses and shutters and such, ah yes, good old Dick never let the grass grow under his feet. By the way, I should add, for whatever it's worth, that the renowned Mr. Detective was in his version of clover at that time. He was carrying on with Karen, whose all-American smile shone through the darkest night, he had a little porno business going with Corrie and Madame Delamode, not to mention their colleague, Annette, specialty poses I think he did for them, *and* also Biff Page had hired him, not really hired, but he worked as a free-lance photographer for Biff's PR agency, and wonder of wonders, will they never cease? one of the first jobs he did was a color layout of Annette's metal apartment that appeared in some ultra-modern house-and-home magazine. Enough to frighten small children. The three fates in their steel peignoirs looking like a dream of the divine Marquis, crackling blaze in the chromium fireplace, aluminum spike heels, and so on. And Annette in those pictures! She'd had something done to her face, plastic surgery probably, or she just *willed* it, it wouldn't surprise me a bit. The point is she didn't look like Annette anymore, she looked like Annie Flammard, not exactly, but as if she were Annie's older sister or maybe even her mother, you know, a really glamorous older woman. She always had looked a little like Annie to begin with, or vice versa. But this was more. It was very unsettling.

Who was Annette Lorpailleur?

Well that's a funny question, I don't mean funny, I mean unexpected, we've talked so much about her, I've talked so much I should say and still here you are still trying to find out, well, I don't *know* what. All I can tell you is what I've already told you, there she was, she just was, she seemed to be in the background for years, but the background *everywhere*, you'd turn around, there was Annette, you know, turn up a damn rock and she'd be looking at you. There were stories about her, oh, endless, one would just cancel out another. You'd hear that she'd been at such and such a place at such and such a time, then the next day you'd hear that no, she couldn't have been there because she was, well, someplace *else*. One story that persisted was that she'd written a novel under the name Ann Redding, supposedly an occult mystery novel, *The Metallic Fly*, that purportedly was really, as they say, a kind of esoteric handbook of demonology for, you know, the initiated, I've never seen a copy, as a matter of fact I checked on the book,

nothing in the card catalogues I checked under that title but there was
an Ann Redding, Ann T. Redding to be exact, but it turned out to be a
book of criticism, literary essays. One I remember was on Cecil, Cecil
Tyrell and Tony Lamont, I can't remember the title, something about
Janus, the Janus something or other, the Janus theme, I don't know. I
just skimmed through it, one of those standard academic essays with
a system, you know? Everything fits into the system or you don't mention it. Bursting with jargon, on and on, the macroparatactics of the
ur-text in self-reflexive surfiction or can microparatactics valorize
the signifier? My point is that the book had a little bio note and a photograph on the jacket, Miss Redding, *Doctor* Redding standing alongside her desk, a lot of books, bookshelves on her right, a window behind her opening onto a garden, a formal English garden, a sunny day,
but Doctor Redding was not, by any stretch of the imagination, Annette Lorpailleur. This woman was in her late thirties or early to mid-
forties, very well groomed, short hair pulled back tight off her face,
tortoiseshell glasses, a tweed suit and tailored blouse, stack-heeled
shoes with small metal buckles, beautiful straight legs, big calves and
very slender ankles, very attractive, like those women in the movies
of the thirties and forties, the anthropologist or professor who takes
off her glasses and unpins her hair and there she is! Lana Turner! Why,
you're, you're b-b-beautiful! some lunk says, Preston Foster or George
Brent. She's carefully, a little stiffly, almost professionally posed, she
has a pen and a sheaf of papers in her hand, there's a little ceramic
mug full of pens and pencils on the desk, a *millefiore* paperweight on
a stack of letters and a small figurine, looks like metal, of some Hindu
god or goddess, I don't know which one, the one that rides a dog,
whoever that is. And this and that, a kind of, what's the word? studied,
right, a kind of studied clutter. Also a little basket of oranges on the
desk. She's very scholarly-looking, attractive, although a little stern,
formidable. The bio note says that she lives just outside London with
her husband, who's a stockbroker. I remember his name, Richard
Gross, Bart., because a few years later he wound up in the papers, his
wife was just mentioned in passing, he was mixed up in some stock-

fraud scheme, involved with a group of people who got insider, confidential information about the market, or he gave this sort of information to other people, it's all kind of vague to me now. That's all by the by, the point is that if Ann T. Redding wrote a novel I couldn't find out about it. And Ann T. Redding was *not* Annette. But that's just one example of the stories, and there were dozens of them, about Annette. Most of them just stayed in the air, just persisted, because nobody could ever find out anything to prove or disprove them. She was strange enough without the stories. O.K. She just left anyway, in a flash, just the way she arrived. And Corrie and Madame Delamode with her. They were supposedly going on a winter cruise to the Bahamas or Bermuda or some damn silly place like that, and they never came back. Their apartment disappeared too, I mean the building it was in, an old brownstone, it got torn down with all the other brownstones on the same side of the street, some sweet real-estate shuffle. The houses were declared undesirable or unsafe or un-some fucking thing or the other, whatever lie was used, down they came and up went these high-rise co-ops, two hundred and fifty grand for three closets and a fireplace just about big enough to burn a popsicle stick. Many bucks, many many bucks were made by somebody. The kind of thing that bastard Biggs Richard would have loved to be in on, except that he'd split too, with, of all people, Lorna Flambeaux, or so we heard. Except that she was by then Lorna Gom, Mrs. Lincoln Gom, maybe I already told you that? She'd become a senior editor and Linc saw the promised land there, he'd never have to work again, right? She must have got fed up with him though, he'd always be bringing home some rocks-and-ferns freak, complete with backpack and sturdy boots, and they almost always turned out to be eighteen- or nineteen-year-old girls, their eyes on the redwoods, their feet in the mud, frogs jumping out of their survival jackets. Well, Lorna just took off, closed out the bank accounts first, and that was that. I think Linc moved in or tried to move in with Lena Schmidt then, gave up the whole ecology con, fuck the whales, right? I don't remember how long that raging love endured but it ended pretty quick. Then, what then? I'm trying to end this whole Lincoln thing, that'll be another thing out of the way, another goddam character. Oh, about Annette, I've got one more story but let me finish with Linc. He kissed every ass in town looking for some kind of a job, you *know* he was desperate, finally he saw some friend who owed Duke Washington a favor, I mean a friend of Duke's. Lincoln had gone to see Duke too. In any event, the friend gave him a job as an assistant to the advance man for a lame heavy-metal band, Dress Rite, spelled r i t e, very cutesy. About a year later they found him dead in a Holiday Inn outside Gallup, o.d.'d on wine and downers. Always the original. Now, Annette, to tell you the last thing I heard about her, supposedly she turned up in Florida somewhere in some retirement community, well, no, not exactly. She had some kind of a partnership with a guy to *develop* retirement villages, little bungalows made out of cardboard and spit, God forbid it should rain, the ceiling would fall down on some poor old guy's head. White Sun Village was the name of the first one as I recall. The thing got blown away in a hurricane and people were hurt, killed, it was in the papers but when the law came to look for Annette, the state or county, whatever, she was long gone. Invisible. It was as if she'd never existed. The papers, the stories in the papers gave her name as something else, some alias, I forget what, but the story going around was that it was in fact Annette. Maybe, maybe not. Nobody's heard anything since about her. For all I know she lives next door, some sophisticated, independent, and mature woman who incidentally owns a couple of hundred tenements crawling with rats. Who knows?

What does the phrase "metallic constructions" mean?

Metallic constructions? I have no idea. I'm sorry, I really can't help you on that one. Metallic constructions. I'm damned if I know.

Why did Bart Kahane tell Leo Kaufman that he had surprised Anne Kaufman and Biff Page on Horace Rosette's bed?

I didn't know that old tale still had any currency because it's absolutely phony, made up out of whole cloth by Bart for the simple purpose of making Anne look bad to Leo. Supposedly it had a lot to do with their marriage finally breaking up, but they were both ready, I mean if it did break the marriage up, it was a thing they grabbed for, something that came along just in time. Anyway, the story went that Biff bumped into Anne one day, this was soon after he'd come back to town after his Baylor Freeq adventures, you'll pardon the expression, but I don't think he'd gone to work for the old man yet, he wasn't yet the *new* Biff, firm of jaw and so on, as if he ever will be, well, they bumped into each other somewhere and had a cup of coffee together. Anne was more or less living with Vance at the time but Vance was broke and a cheap son of a bitch as well, so she had no money and was looking for a job. She hadn't met Tony yet, I don't think so anyway, it wouldn't have mattered, since he wouldn't have given her any money even if he had some, it all went right over the bar. Leo was spending as much time as he could with Ellen, his little Eskimo Pie, eating her oven-fried okra and chicken-guts Madeira with marshmallows and spanking her every day and twice on Sundays, love in full bloom. It makes me laugh when I think that Ellen became a firebrand in the feminist movement, fedora and all, overalls for Christ sake. She probably started to make speeches because she couldn't sit down. Well that's neither here nor there. My point is that Leo spent the few shekels he could get his mitts on on Ellen, though her brother Jack used to give her an allowance. So. Biff and Anne got to talking and he mentioned that she had probably heard that he and Barnett had opened a restaurant together, a chic, overpriced seafood joint that they called Les Lobsters, cute as a little button, one of those traps with the lobsters in tanks so you could pick your own, as if you're, you know, exercising your shellfish expertise, the carafes of house white and red, the crudités and rice pilaf, all the young blond fag waiters who were *really* actors and dancers, what else would they be? And the Mozart cassettes and so on, the works. To sit down and have a glass of water you dropped five bucks, when they brought you a menu, or I should say when Allen or Chet or Dwight or Ronnie brought you a menu you said goodbye to another fin. Well, the upshot of this was that they needed a hostess, an attractive woman who'd look good in clothes, someone to say hello, seat people, you know the things they do. O.K., Anne thought it was great, she could make a few bucks for herself and get out from under Leo *and* Vance, right? So she says it sounds great and—this was the story—they go up to Horace's place because Horace supposedly wanted to introduce Biff to some starving painter who did little watercolors of lobsters and crabs and fish that Biff might be interested in buying, or commissioning, to hang on the walls of Les Lobsters, the deluxe touch, sure. Horace was out but Biff had a key, a lot of people had keys to Horace's place, and they sat down to wait, have a smoke, one thing led to another and they wound up in the sack. Enter Bart Kahane, who was sucking around Horace at the time so that he could meet what he thought of as important people, the poor deluded bastard, Horace was no doubt making him perform unnatural acts in spades, you know? Bend over, Bart, my boy, we'll while away the time until David Rockefeller arrives to discuss off-shore oil leasing. So in barges Bart and catches Anne and Biff in flagrante on the bed, he rushes out and tells his old pal, Leo. What are friends for? The only thing true about this bullshit story is that Anne was indeed in bed naked but *not* with Biff Page. You've got to understand that Bart really hated Anne because when she and Leo started to drift apart, I love that phrase, Anne was falling into bed with everybody, including a few women, making a few trios and quartets as well, but she wouldn't give Bart a tumble. She just thought he was a clown. I personally heard her say to him once, she was three sheets to the wind, she told him that she didn't want to make it with him because she was terrified that she'd die laughing. I don't know, something about the guy even then just turned her permanently off, and then, oh yeah, then just before this alleged incident with Biff she began to call Bart Les, you know, short for Lester, because he'd thought up the name Les Lobsters and Barnett gave him, I don't know, ten or twenty bucks in appreciation, and he took it! Then everybody picked up on this nickname and poor Bart got to be *known* as Les, some people were even *introduced* to him that way. So there was no love lost between Bart and Anne Kaufman, believe me. But the real story behind Bart's telling Leo about Anne was very different. Barnett really had the hots for Anne and Biff told her this story, which was true, in a way, they did need a hostess, but I suspect that Barnett had Léonie in mind for the job, but who knows? Biff told her, as I say, this story, then asked her to go up to Horace's to meet the fish artist, and who should be there? You've got it, Barnett, all by his lonesome, knocking back the sauce and getting himself into a lather. He'd had this mad lust for Anne ever since a Halloween costume party that Annette and friends had given that year to which Anne had come as a baby. She wore a white bra and a *diaper*. I mean it was really weird, I think she did it to out-weird Annette, Corrie, and the Madame, who were dressed like store mannequins, made up that way, and they moved in these little jerks as if they were robots. Well when Barnett got an eyeful of Anne in her baby costume he got crazy because he knew, as did everyone else, that Leo used to like to spank Anne and he must have put this together in his diseased mind with the diaper. To tell the truth, maybe Anne did it because she knew that Leo had told everyone anyway and she figured what the hell, bring it out in the open. I don't know. That was another sparkling trait that Leo had, he'd tell you anything about himself, the most personal things, right out of the blue, the son of a bitch had no shame at all. Every hopeless drunk within a radius of twenty miles knew every excruciating detail of Leo's sex life with Anne, he should have sent it to the newspapers. As a matter of fact, when he started going around with Ellen he'd take you by the lapels and give you a play-by-play of *their* personal lives, or he'd walk into whatever bar everybody was hanging out in and show you things he'd bought for her from the Soirée Intime, with her money of course, for their, what did he call them? I don't remember, something like erotic nocturnes, whatever. Or he'd show you his lotions and creams and ointments, once he even passed a French tickler around, the man was astonishing. But I'm getting away from, right, so Biff takes Anne up to Horace's, there's Barnett, Biff leaves posthaste, and Anne is in the sack with *Barnett* when Bart walks in. Bart rushes out to tell Leo this tale, but changing Barnett to Biff. O.K. He was avenging himself on Anne because, as I said, she would never give him the time of day, but he was also protecting his ass. Bart didn't dare tell Leo that Barnett was shtupping Anne because Barnett had already made, to put it delicately, veiled threats against Bart's life and limb, Jesus, these things are all coming back to me, what a mess. It seems, or the rumor was, that Barnett was sleeping regularly with Lolita, who at that time had been married to Bart about a month, they're divorced now, as I told you. Now, Conchita told Barnett that she knew that he was getting his ashes hauled regularly by Lolita and Barnett figured that Bart knew and had told Conchita, his usual crying-in-his-beer routine, right? But Bart, as far as I know, had no idea that Lolita was two-timing him. At any rate, Barnett called Bart up and told him that he wasn't at all pleased that his name had been linked with Lolita, did Bart think that he, a man in his position, had to sneak around with married women? Then he said that if he heard, from anyone at all, any more stories that mentioned his name in an insulting or demeaning way, Bart would find himself involved in, ah, unpleasantries, that's the kind of word that Tete would use. Then he mentioned, oh so casually, the high-heels kid, Roger Whytte-Blorenge, you remember, woddayasay kid yawanna get some ersters? O.K. Roger worked for Pungoe, worked, well, did this and that, dirty work I suppose you'd call it, but Pungoe and Tete were sometime business associates, to coin a euphemism, the story was that at this time they were ripping off designer dresses and selling them, selling the designs, to ready-to-wear clothing manufacturers before the models in Paris and Milan and New York had even modeled them, don't ask me, some racket they were in cahoots on, there was a rumor that Pungoe and Tete had paid a bundle of money to have some kind of mini-camera fitted into a special pair of glasses, you know, eyeglasses, that somebody in the fashion business, or probably more than one someone, but people in their employ, you'll pardon the expression, would use to photograph the big designers' new lines. I'm ignorant of that business so I don't know if it could have been possible to do that, I do know though that the both of them were walking around at that time looking like the cat who ate the canary. Anyway, Roger the shoe fetishist was a certified thug, and Barnett suggested that old Rog might pay

Bart a visit if and when he heard, etcetera, etcetera. So Bart just substituted Biff for Tete and got even, so to speak, with Anne. But she didn't give a good goddam, as I said, this was what got the divorce started. To the satisfaction of all parties.

Is it possible that Conchita had learned of Lolita's indiscretions with Mr. Tete through Bart?

I'd say that it was possible but highly unlikely, improbable. When Lolita and Tete were having their fling Conchita was in Paris, and I can't imagine Bart calling her up to tell her or even, for that matter, writing her. But *somebody* told her, unless the whole story about her telling Tete that she knew is suspect, if there was anything *to* know. Which happens to be my own opinion, that is, that there was nothing to know. I mean to say that I think Lolita still really loved Bart in some odd way, and I mean odd, at the time and I don't think she would have become involved with Barnett and if she was involved certainly Conchita wouldn't have given a damn, she wouldn't have told Tete that she knew. I'm afraid that I can't explain all this clearly, but you should understand that most of these people were more or less reasonably all right until odd things started to happen, odd people started to, I don't know. I mean people like Barnett and Pungoe, you know, Roger, Annette Lorpailleur and her two friends, when they suddenly appeared it was as if a kind of disease infected everybody, people got crazy, weird, they got foul and greedy and mean. I told you about Léonie, for instance, who was a lovely young woman and who became a drunken bitch, and of course Jack Towne, Tania, oh God, it all happened over a few years really. Well. Lolita loved Bart, O.K. Now maybe she did sleep with Barnett, Bunny said that she saw him once every two weeks for an evening, he'd take her to dinner then go home with her, she'd stay the night, five hundred dollars. This may or may not be true, maybe Lolita *was* just a whore, I don't know. It would have been better than putting up with Cecil Tyrell's shit when she was nursing him through that goddam novel of his, *Orange Steel*, and supporting him as well, getting an occasional shot in the chops for her trouble. But what Bunny had to say should be taken very carefully, because

Bunny had no love for Lolita then, although they live together now, or they did a few months or so back. So I heard. But at that time she had a suspicion that Lolita and Guy were lovers, a real mistake! If there was someone that Lolita hated it was Guy Lewis, this dated from the night at somebody's place, I think I mentioned this, maybe the Lewises', when Lolita was in the bathroom and Guy walked in on her and just stood there smoking a cigarette and grinning like an ape, watching her. Bunny figured they were up to some funny business in there and so if she passed the word around that Lolita was a whore, Barnett's whore, it wouldn't surprise me if it was all just an invention. And of course now, if you ask anybody about this, anybody who was around at the time, it's a *fact*, I mean, sure, Lolita and Guy were lovers. It's carved in stone. An interesting sidelight on this is that in *Synthetic Ink* there's a strange scene in which one of his characters, somebody named Daisy, is involved in some kinky sex in a bathroom with a demented soldier, a deserter I think. He ties her to the toilet with her stockings, she loves it, then you discover that this is really just one of Daisy's lecherous fantasies. Tony got a lot of grief from Ellen Kaufman about that scene when she became a militant feminist, she was the vice-president of some group that boycotted bookstores and so on, Tony was so constantly stoned in those days he probably thought they were loyal fans clamoring to buy his book and meet the author, but my point is that the woman in the novel, Daisy, was modeled on Lolita, whom Tony despised, because he thought, rightly or wrongly, that Lolita and Lee Jefferson were buddies and he hated Lee too. This, by the way, I mean Lolita being used as the model for Daisy, is, according to some people, why *Hip Vox* went out of its way to kick the hell out of *Synthetic Ink*, that assault by John Hicks I told you about? Maybe so, but that would imply that Lee and Lolita were indeed friends, I don't know about that, I think personally it was because Lee was, you know, up-to-the-minute Charlie and she knew that it would go over big with the *Hip Vox* audience to savage Tony's novel, feminism was just then becoming a valuable commodity, it sold, if you'll pardon my cynicism. I'm *still* not making my point. My point, Jesus, my point being that people who knew that Daisy was based on Lolita thought that the bathroom scene was, you know, *actual*, that it was the way *Lolita* really was, they believed the goddam novel. People are really amazing, can you imagine believing a novel? So Lolita suffered and all the others involved were delighted, Ellen and her radical-feminist group, I can't remember their name, got a lot of mileage out of it, Lee added a lot of new subscribers, even Tony got a kind of backhanded push with the publicity, some interviews and such, a talk show, he even made a pretty respectable paperback deal, I can remember the cover they did, bright red with the title and his name spelled out in letters drawn to look like stockings, black nylon stockings, and a little banner printed across the bottom, The blistering novel that enraged the women of America! Beautiful. And for the next year or so every time Lolita got up to go to the bathroom at a party or in a bar somebody would pass a smart remark, that lunk Doctor Plot, you know, Page Moses, even threw her a salute once. She spit in his face.

Why did Lolita Kahane slap Conchita?

That's news to me. If she did I never heard about it, although it sounds like the kind of story that Bart might have made up to make it look as if these two women were fighting, you know, over him. Very unlikely. Lolita and Conchita got along pretty well as a matter of fact, for a time they even went to the same hair stylist, bought their clothes at the same stores, they even showed up at one of Pungoe's parties dressed exactly alike. I don't know if that was accidental or not, but. However, you might be interested to know that Lolita slapped *some* woman at a little bar that Barry Gatto worked in as night manager, a place called The Black Basement, this was some time after Barry and Annie Flammard were divorced and he needed a job. Annie and Buffie Tate, with the help of Annette, gave him the business in the home-decorating racket they'd been in, they got some other guy to take Barry's place, Serge something or other, and the great part about it was that this loser had an ear that had even more tin in it than Barry's, it was beyond belief. Anyway, a bunch of us went to this trap, The Black Basement, one night right after Barry got the job, it was somewhere to hell and gone, and some dump. There must have been about ten of us there and what happens is that Sister Rose, Rose Zeppole? comes up to the table where Lolita is sitting and starts telling her that she, Lolita, would be perfect in a new movie that Rose was going to start shooting in a few weeks, a blue movie of course, and Rose is saying that she's exactly right for the part, they're looking for a woman to play the role of a nymphomaniac business executive, executrix? whatever. Lolita was turning colors but Rose was so sincere that she didn't know what to say, I mean that was the strange thing about Rose. She was somehow sweet, innocent, despite the dirty movies she made a living in. She'd made *Sisters in Shame* and then, in a row, three flicks called *The Party*, *Chorus Orgy*, and *Silk Sighs*, and by this time, the night I'm talking about, she was a kind of chic celebrity. This came about mainly because of an essay that Saul Blanche wrote on her for *Big Apple*, a serious piece, or it *looked* serious, Saul wrote it straight-faced anyway. As I recall, it went on about the sense of existential dread in Rose's films, and her strange innocence, right, she was innocent the way Sade's Justine is innocent and because of her beauty and purity she's always being seduced or ravished or defiled by the men she meets and this happens over and over again, she never learns anything, she's too good to learn anything from evil, Saul used the phrase accidental body, I think. In other words, let me see now, it went that Rose had a body that was beautiful, voluptuous, sensual, but it was a kind of betrayal of her mind, of her essential morality. Her body got her, you know, into all these perverse scenes. The upshot was that she was a kind of innocent sex-goddess, Saul threw Marilyn Monroe in, *The Perils of Pauline*, *Dracula*, everything but the kitchen sink. Rose became an underground star, if you were hip, you know, you'd *have* to have seen Rose's flicks. It became fashionable and perfectly respectable for a whole party of people to go and see one of Rose's movies after dinner, that sort of thing. There was even talk that people would go to somebody's place after seeing one of Rose's movies and re-enact scenes from it, I remember that they called these gatherings, these orgies, rose parties or rose gardens. The big movie was *Sisters in*

Shame, Saul gave that one a lot of space. Rose played a nun so all of Saul's ideas were brought into focus in that flick, they even ran the son of a bitch at a couple of art-film festivals. Anyway, anyway, what was I? Right, Lolita and the woman she slapped, O.K. Rose was at Barry's place with a woman nobody had ever seen before, maybe about thirty, early thirties, and she just sat there and smiled while Rose was giving her pitch to Lolita. As I said, Lolita was absolutely nonplussed but she had no idea how to handle it because it was so obvious that Rose had no intention of insulting her. Then just as Rose is explaining the financial arrangements that Lolita can expect to make with the guy who's going to make the film, this woman looks at Lolita and then at Rose and says something that sounds like, I don't know, sounds like nothing, gibberish, incomprehensible, and she's making gestures with her hands. Lolita thought she'd insulted her or was making fun of her, I don't know, and she hauls off and gives this woman a slap that almost knocked her off her chair. The woman starts to cry and then Rose is crying and yelling at Lolita, she's really upset, and believe me, Rose was a great cryer, there wasn't a movie she made that she didn't cry in, this was also, I should add, a very big item in Saul's essay. Well, to cut it short, it turns out that this woman, an old friend of Rose's, was deaf and dumb and that what Lolita thought was an insult was this woman just, you know, trying to say something and using sign language and it also turns out that what she was trying to say was that she thought that Rose was embarrassing Lolita. That's what Rose was screaming at Lolita. Then *Lolita* started to cry. Barry was running around like a crazy man, figuring that this was the end of his job almost before it started. As it happened, though, Rose and Lolita and Rose's friend all calmed down and spent the rest of the evening together, thick as thieves.

What were Bart Kahane's motives in following Sheila Henry into the bathroom?

I really can't say, motives, God only knows what motives Bart had for doing anything, he'd started to go around the bend after he and Conchita split up or right after he married Lolita, I can't remember precisely. He followed Sheila into the bathroom in the Caliph's Walk, not The Black Basement. As I recall, Bart went into the happy house some time before The Black Basement even opened, so it would definitely have been in the Caliph's Walk. Bart was working there as the bartender, no, wait a minute, as a waiter, it was soon after Guy Lewis got canned for tapping the till for a pound here and a pound there, not that he really needed the money, he was all set by then with Pungoe in the mail-order scheme. Bart said that he followed Sheila in because he wanted to tell her that the toilet didn't flush, but that was a lie, the toilet flushed fine. Sheila gave him a smack across the face and came out of the ladies' room just boiling. It was no secret that Bart was wild about Sheila and he probably had some idea that Sheila kind of liked him too. Where he got that idea nobody knew, Sheila was all innocence, she just said he was weird, you know, kinky, which seemed to wash, because Marcie Butler had told me and a few other people that Bart used to buy the kind of perfume she wore, expensive stuff called Ce Soir, and put it on his pillow and his underwear and under his arms and he was, you know, *serious* about it. I mean that if somebody said, you know, how wonderful he smelled or something like, say, Bart, how about the two of us flying into the night together, you sweetie, it wasn't funny, was *not* funny to him at all. He'd look in your goddam face and say, this is Ce Soir, Marcella's scent. And with these blank screwball's eyes staring straight at you. He also had, Marcie said, a drawerful of women's hankies, little linen handkerchiefs with a lace trim, all of them scented with this perfume. He used to have long talks with Sheila about *her* perfume, tried to get her to use Ce Soir, he gave her these handkerchiefs, you know, he'd say, here, carry this for a while and see how much you'll get to love this scent. I think that Sheila was maybe touched, if that's the word, but she couldn't take him seriously, especially after people started to call him Les. Poor bastard then occasionally started to answer to the name, which didn't exactly put him in the role of a Valentino, if you get what I mean. On top of all this he was a bum waiter, fucked up the orders, spilled soup, kept people waiting forever for the check, most of the time because he was on the phone to Lolita, I guess, arguing with her. Sometimes he'd start to cry and there he'd be, right? slapping down some poor bastard's shrimp cocktail with the tears streaming down his face and the smell of perfume off him like a Mexican whorehouse. Anyway, all this is just by way of preface to why Bart wound up in the nuthouse.

It is?

Yeah. Bart had a lot of problems as long as I knew him. He was a really brilliant guy, the type that could beat you at chess while he read a book, you know? Mathematics, physics, they were really his meat, but he just couldn't get it together, he married Conchita when he was just a kid, she was too, and he dropped out of college, graduate school, then started making a buck doing theses and dissertations for people. The thing that really wrecked him, or so Lolita said, was that he wrote a Ph.D. dissertation on some complicated math problem for some joker and in it he put all his own ideas, all his own original thinking. I'm saying that what he did was write *his* dissertation and sell it to some guy. And the saddest part of it all is that he did it so he could buy some new furniture for Conchita, they were living in a goddam basement at the time, sitting on these chairs the Salvation Army wouldn't even take off your hands, you know? So he buys a couch and a couple of easy chairs, a coffee table, the usual stuff. Conchita is delighted, but when she finds out where Bart got the money that was really that, it was, I don't know, it was contemptible to her, she started to treat Bart *so* badly. When they had people over Bart would, you know, serve. I don't mean that he'd help out or that he and Conchita would work together, host and hostess, no, Conchita would act as if she'd, I don't know how to put it, as if she'd *hired* him. And one night, one night damned if he didn't serve the whole night wearing an apron and a maid's cap, you know, those frilly little caps with the ribbons? Even Conchita did a double take. And that's how it went from then on, she humiliated him and he humiliated himself, she even took to calling him Berthe in front of guests, visitors, anybody. But Bart *liked* it. Anyway, when he met Lolita she didn't know about this and Bart came on like Jack Armstrong, Mr. Manly Normal, mm-hm. After they were married things must have got hairy, it turned out, I heard from Tania, who heard from Lucy Taylor, *all* the women knew about it, that Bart was impotent unless he played the woman's role. When they made love. Lolita was so upset by this that she didn't know what to do so she started to buy these fancy things, fancy underwear from Soirée Intime to seduce Bart, but it turned out that *he* wanted to wear them. She went along even with this but then he starts nagging her about her dressing like a *man*. That was it. Lolita was devastated, there was no way around it if she wanted sex, I was going to say if she wanted a normal sex life, ho ho ho. To be absolutely crude, he couldn't get it up at all unless they were in each other's clothes, so to speak. This was when he started to wear the Ce Soir, I guess. Must have been. Well. One night at a party Bart was so drunk he could hardly talk, it turned out that earlier in the day Lolita had told him she was going to leave him, at least for a while, you know, to think things out because it all seemed so impossible, and so on. At the party Lolita started to carry on with, of all people, Roger, making a fool of herself, dancing with him and rubbing up against him, she was pretty well sauced herself. Bart is sitting there knocking back the booze and getting drunker by the minute. All of a sudden that goddam pig, Sol Blanc, starts to laugh and point and holler, then everybody looks and Bart's sock, the poor bastard, his sock has slipped down and you can see that he's got nylons, nylon stockings on under the socks. Well, the jokes and the cracks and the hoots and hollers, the place sounds like a rally for Jesus and the grand old flag put together. Bart gets up, the poor miserable bastard, he gets up and pulls his pants off, he's wearing these nylon stockings, women's underwear, and he stands there, he's spitting at people, he's cursing and crying and swinging his arms around, Jesus! Lolita starts to go over to him, she's crying too, and the poor bastard, the poor bastard turns around and just jumps out the window, we're two stories up. He broke his arm and his collarbone, got a concussion, and they took him away to the hospital. From there to the psychiatric ward for observation. Then he was committed. By Lolita. It was really grim, a really grim night.

Who was at the party? All the names.

Oh come on. You're asking me the impossible. I can remember most of the people, but *all* the names? I don't know if I've made it clear but you know that these were parties that attracted all kinds of people, anybody. Some ace from Christ knows where would hear about a party sitting in some bar and he'd show up with all his friends. I'll do my best. I was there but I didn't want to be, I wasn't getting on too well with certain people at the time and I knew they'd be there. Ted Buckie-Moeller, it was his housewarming, you might say it was a spurious housewarming since Ted was subletting a loft for six months, it wasn't, strictly speaking, his place. He was one of the people I wasn't getting along with by the way, he'd run out on me as it were, we were sharing a shotgun flat and he got this sublet and left me with all the bills to pay, rent and gas and electricity and such on the dump and he didn't want me to move in with him because he'd started an affair with Tania at the time, we were supposed to be married in a couple of months and she just gave me the business. Well. O.K. And Bart and Lolita, Roger, Sol Blanc, right, I told you about that fat fool, and Saul Blanche and Marcie, they were still an item in those days before Saul discovered that he was twisted, if you ask me I think he was a phony, I mean he decided to admit that he was gay because it was getting to be sort of hip, you know? O.K. Harlan, Annette, I think maybe Corrie and Madame Delamode, Annie Flammard, Tony Lamont, ZuZu, you know, Lee Jefferson, and I think maybe Henri Kink, but that may be just my imagination. Then there were the usual crashers, drunks and junkies and lames and losers looking for free booze and whatever the hell else was free, and three guys that I found out had been invited, they were supposed to be film makers or some goddam film something, as a matter of fact I believe they were the guys who made the Sister Rose flick, *The Party*. They made a barrel of money on it, so I heard, and Rose, as usual, got screwed, pardon the pun. One guy was supposed to be a hot avant-garde Italian movie genius, I think his name was Tucci or Tucco, Tuccio? I don't recall but he looked like a standard corner deadbeat to me, maybe that was his style, you've got me. He was wearing this old forties-style suit, a one-button lounge they used to call them, pearl gray with white chalk stripes, a white-on-white shirt, a knitted tie and black French-toe shoes. The other two partners I can barely remember, one was a tall dark guy with a big hooked nose who spoke really weird English and the other was an old man with white hair and a beat-up Panama hat, he looked like the classic stereotype of the down-and-out beachcomber, right? I remember that clearly because it struck me that this guy was missing on a couple of cylinders, it was the middle of winter, as a matter of fact it was snowing that night, right, poor old Bart was lying in the snow when we ran down to see how hurt he was. What made me think that these three were just assholes, outside of the fact that they looked like the Three Stooges, was that the old guy with the straw hat was carrying this big bundle wrapped in newspaper, it turned out that it was the manuscript of some monster novel and he spent most of the night trying to get Saul to take the goddam thing for a reading. As far as I know that was it except for, as I said, except for the mobs that came and went looking for some action. To tell you the truth, all I *really* remember is that moment when Bart went out the window, screaming and crying. God. I'll tell you the truth, it didn't bother me a bit when I found out that somebody dropped the dime on Sol Blanc with the immigration people and got the prick deported. That was much later though, I'm way ahead of myself, Sol was getting greedy, greedier by the day, and he tried to muscle in on some prostitution scam that Jack Marowitz had going, some kind of dating-service hustle, Jack was in on this with Annie Flammard and Lorna too for that matter, it was called Marquise Meetings, Inc. That was Lorna's fine Italian hand. The classified copy was something else. It ran along the lines of, Marquise Meetings, Inc. Are you tired of dates that center on dull, I think they said vapid, on vapid talk of TV, Hollywood, and the so-called adventures of the so-called famous? Talk about pop music, chic restaurants, and Broadway theatre? And best-sellers, this and that, a few more things, fashion. MMI has beautiful, intelligent young hostesses whose conversation will refresh your sense of the truly sophisticated. Some crap like that, what it meant was that some whore had a little ten-minute line about Picasso or Eliot or somebody that she'd give the john before she got down to business. And oh yes, Cecil Tyrell was also at the party, he got into a beef with Tony over something dumb, some writer's thing, all I can recall of that is Cecil standing there, about a quart of vodka in him, saying over and over, What's the fucking exegesis? What's the fucking exegesis? Christ only knows what he was talking about. And Tony is sitting there with a book open saying, Thirty-three times three, thirty-three times three, you goddam idiot, thirty-three times three! Oh it was really a moonlight-and-roses night.

Why were you invited to this party?

Well to tell you the truth I wasn't *really* invited. I certainly wasn't invited by Ted, I think he was surprised when I showed up but he didn't say anything, Tania was embarrassed, that was in the days before she was incapable of being embarrassed, before she became one of the important people. Anyway, I thought that I had to go to see if I could do Guy a favor, he'd asked me to talk to Pungoe about maybe getting that job, you know? The mail-order thing? Wait a minute. This is a little complicated, let me spell it out. I was on fairly close terms, business terms, if you'll pardon the expression, with Harlan then. I'd recommended a couple of hard-up artists to him, he wanted some artists to do some wood-block prints for him. As I recall he wanted to decorate the rooms in some hotel or motel outside the city that he had part interest in and he didn't want the usual horses and trees and dogs and views of Venice, you know the garbage they put on the walls. Anyway, we worked a deal out, he'd pay the artists for the prints and give me ten percent of what he paid them, a sort of finder's fee, I was like an agent, a middleman. It wasn't much money, especially since Harlan often screwed me, but it kept me going, I didn't have much more of an income, really just some money I'd saved. From the days when I was making a lot of money, very good money. Harlan wasn't exactly all heart, or all business for that matter, he really had his eye on Tania, so it turned out. What he wanted was for me to make him look good to Tania, you know, the art connoisseur. I was too dumb to know it but as it turned out even if I'd wanted to, or even if I knew what Harlan wanted, she and Ted had already made their plans. For all I know he got *Ted* to do his work for him, because right after she and Ted moved into this loft she started managing Tete's boutique, almost as if, well, almost as if he and Pungoe had made an arrangement to share her. But I haven't got any proof as to what happened or what didn't. It's all water under the bridge anyway, I don't give a goddam anymore. Well. To get back to Guy, I thought I'd do him this favor and tell Harlan what a hell of a guy he was, a good worker, ambitious, he really needed the money, was he supposed to work for bar tips all his life and so on. I owed Guy this, a lot more really because, well. Because, you see, I used to make a lot of money working for a company that made TV commercials, a fairly small film-production company that did work for ad agencies. I started out taking Polaroid shots of locations, possible locations, that the producer and director could look at to see if they were O.K. to shoot at. For instance, if the commercial was going to be for, let's say corn flakes, and they wanted some all-American schmuck to be eating this shit in the back yard of a typical American house in the suburbs, a typical American suburban street, I'd go out with my camera to a few suburbs and take fifty, a hundred pictures. Then they'd pick the best one, or I should say one that was most in keeping with the sanctity of the product and the show would be on the road. Anyway, one thing led to another, in a year and a half I was an assistant producer with a card yet, and making a lot of money, oh the money they spend in that racket is enough to make you weep. I traveled all over the world, thirty-second spot on a street in Madrid, by Jesus, swarms of people, tons of equipment, everyone and everything went first class to Spain for a whole week. For thirty seconds! Jesus Christ. What I remember from all this is the bars and restaurants and rooms in about a hundred Hiltons. They all look alike, you're having a drink in Paris and you might as well be in Florence or Pittsburgh for Christ sake. Well, it all started to get me down, you know? I couldn't sleep, I started in on the sauce pretty good, lots of uppers, lots of downers, a little coke, you name it. The thing that really cut it was one time we were doing some job for an agency that had a cat-food account. Some genius, a creative director, can you imagine that, they call these scumbags creative directors? These bastards used to sit around and talk about the best way for an actor to hold a roll of toilet paper, the most aesthetic and *convincing* way. These people were serious, I'm not kidding you, *serious* about their useless fucking lives. Anyway. Some creative afterbirth got the idea, I can't recall this too well, I was spaced out day and night then, he got the idea of building this commercial around the notion that cats loved this swill so much that they'd swim to get to it. So we had a bunch of poor goddam cats that we'd throw up in the air and into a swimming pool, they put little swim caps on them, Jesus Christ! Two guys threw them into this pool over and over and over again, they'd *blow-dry* them, a special creative blow-dry team, in the poor little fucks would go again, they were absolutely traumatized, and they'd film away and film away till the director got what he wanted. They had the usual guy from the humane society, right? but they paid him off or somebody gave him a blow job so he'd be sure to keep his mouth shut. So I said, I don't know, what the hell am I doing in this filthy shit and I started to really hit the sauce, I mean *serious* boozing. Then I woke up one morning and I sort of saw myself setting fire to the curtains as if I was somebody else. Then I started to shake. I mean I sort of went around the bend a little, right? So I went away for a while, well, with the help of a shrink I put myself into a sanitarium. I was in this place for about two months, getting straight and drying out, I should tell you that I'd been seeing Marcie before I went away and when I came out she was living with Saul. Well. I don't blame her, our last few months together she might as well have been sleeping with a zombie, I was the living dead, believe me. Anyway, Guy comes in here, I'm sorry to lay all this sorry business on you, Guy comes in here because when I got out he asked me if I'd like to move in with him and Bunny till I got straightened out. So, you know, I owed him. He was a good friend and so was Bunny. The terrible part of it all was that I fell for Bunny, it was mutual, really, but we just, we just *looked* at each other. It was strictly hands off. I wanted her so desperately but for Christ sake! I was in her *house, Guy's* house. He was oblivious, he trusted me, so. Well I got the hell out of there as soon as I could and took a job with, of all people, Annette Lorpailleur, she'd settled in and wanted somebody to do the cleaning and the shopping, wash the clothes, a kind of housekeeper, but she didn't want to hire a woman. She said to me that although men pried as much as women did, men didn't hold what they found out against you. That's neither here nor there. I made her her coffee in the morning, sometimes lunch when she was at home, never dinner. She was always either out or she'd hire a cook when she was having guests. She wasn't so weird then or maybe I just didn't notice, I was really hanging on. Just hanging on. That's how I first got to know Pungoe, through Annette. But at this particular time, the housewarming, things were rather chilly between Pungoe and me since I'd found out about him and Bunny, all that perverse business with her, so I wasn't feeling any too warm toward him although I'm ashamed to say that I didn't let it interfere with our little business arrangement, maybe I should say that *I* was cool toward Harlan but I didn't let him know that I knew. I didn't let Bunny or Guy know either. I kept it to myself. I'll tell you though that it cured me of my feelings for Bunny, when I found out I just felt sorry for her and for Guy too, really, they were caught, you know, just boxed in by circumstances. I've thought about it since. I've thought about it, I mean maybe I *should* have told Guy about it, but what good would it have done? He found out himself later anyway and it didn't help anything. I wish that I hadn't been told about it at all, it was April who spilled the famous beans. Who else? When it came to scandals, especially those involving sex, April was the daily news, she was *everywhere.* I told you about the time that Tania and I were smoking some grass in a bedroom at a dinner party and there was April banging on the door to tell us some dirt she'd found out about somebody, Léonie I think, and Lucy Taylor, who were supposed to be lovers, they used the back of Barnett's boutique where Léonie worked for their rendezvous. April loved it. So, in any event, I went to the damn party and put in a word for Guy with Harlan but I'm sorry I went because I think that I was responsible for

Bart jumping out the window. Well, indirectly. Guy had really got me mad because he was ignoring Bunny, she was miserable, but, you know, I had to play it very cool, not seem to be interfering, had I known then that they were married the way, I mean that their marriage was a joke, maybe I would have felt differently. I don't know. But I was in a sour mood. Guy was feeling his oats because Pungoe had more or less told him that the job looked good, he was in, this was after I spoke to Harlan but the son of a bitch never even thanked me, well, O.K. There was Bunny, drunk and making a fool of herself sprawled in a chair with her legs wide open and her skirt too high, a cigarette hanging out of her mouth, she looked like some fucking tramp off the street, spilling her drink all over the front of her dress. And then I got into an argument with Sol, I hated the bastard, the only thing that Annie Flammard and I ever agreed on was Sol. He was sort of the rage according to some precious, some arty little magazine, a faggy photography magazine, what was its name? I can't, oh yes, *Filter Blue*, Christ! The jerk was a Neanderthal, I mean he took pictures the way any slob in the street takes pictures, aim and shoot, he didn't know dick-all about anything. *Filter Blue*'s editor thought he was just too, too charming, right? So, you know, unaffected, so crude, so honest, so cruelly blunt, so *primitive*. Sol's shtick was to take these crummy snapshots of derelicts, bums, drunks, beat-up old ladies. It was sickening to me, a kind of brutal exploitation. So I started to needle him about the travails of being an artist, especially a foreign artist in a crass and philistine country and he took it out on Bart. I ought to add, as long as I'm telling you about Guy, it really got to me that he was the one who laughed loudest at Bart. I figured, at that moment, I didn't owe him another goddam thing. When I think about it I'm sorry now that I didn't give him the horns. Well, maybe he got what he deserved anyway because later he took the fall for Pungoe and Annette on a mail-fraud rap.

Was Guy Lewis married?

Yes, sure, they were married. If you mean, I guess you mean were they legally married, that I don't know, I don't think so. I think

that Bunny was always a lesbian, she had a long and very passionate
affair with Lorna Flambeaux and she did her damnedest to put the
make on Sheila, she probably succeeded, and there was a time there
when it was really embarrassing to see. Bunny would get a few in her
and she'd start, in front of anybody, I mean *anybody*, to rub up against
Sheila, feel her breasts, put her hands up her skirt, try to kiss her. It
was really incredible. Sheila went through her patented no-no-no routine for the usual three seconds. The deal with Guy or so I gathered
later from Lucy after she and Bunny went their separate ways, was
that when Bunny got away from Harlan she asked her parents for
some money for an apartment till she could get a job and so on, her
parents weren't too happy with her, right? They were solid suburban
citizens and were upset when Bunny dropped out of college. Anyway.
She asked them for money for a place, said she was going to go back
to school and get her degree, sure sure, but they'd had it with Bunny,
then she met Guy and he went out to their place, Katydid Glade, Gnat-
ville, whatever, some classic burg, row houses with the little crabgrass
lawns and the barbecue pits and the petitions against through traffic,
the works. So she said they were going to be married and Guy gave
them some line of crap about working in the restaurant business, he
modestly told them of his dream of owning his own place some day,
how much he loved children, the need for a strong America, how he
was sick and tired of foreigners taking advantage of us, *us* he said, you
could hear the violins. So they came up with a few grand for their
daughter's new leaf, right? And said they'd give her a little allowance
to boot. But as I said, the deal was that Bunny wanted to live alone and
have a clear field with women but she couldn't lay this on mom and
pop, she had to come on like Miss Cover Girl. I often used to wonder
what her parents would have said if they'd got a look at some of Harlan's photographs of Miss Cover Girl and two rednecks looking like a
bag of pretzels. The old man's clip-on sunglasses would have melted
right into the birdbath. But there was no way that they were going to
give her any bread unless they thought she was settling down. That's
where Guy came in. The problem was that Guy knew that Bunny

wasn't going to marry him but he had no idea that Bunny was a dyke, as a matter of fact the whole thing looked sweet as sugar to him. I mean Bunny was not, as they say, hard to look at and she had a gorgeous body. Then when the whole thing was settled and the money was in the bag, Bunny starts in with Lorna, then with this woman and that one, her great passion for Sheila. Then Lucy sort of moved in. It must have been like living in a sorority house for Guy, not that I feel bad for him, though I admit I did at the time. I was ignorant of Bunny's proclivities then too, Guy, give him credit, didn't say a word, in fact a few people had it figured that Guy was the one who was carrying on with Lorna, you know? The first time I had an idea, well, an *idea*, it was more than an idea, of what was really happening, was one night in some bar when Bunny and Lucy had a lovers' quarrel, it was after Annette had arrived and I'd already, I think, started working for her. Annette and Lucy were talking and laughing together in a booth, one of those big circular booths, there were about seven or eight people around the table and Bunny just suddenly flew off the handle, told Lucy that she wasn't used to being ignored by dowdy little sluts like her and she climbed over two or three people and was out of the place in a flash. The veils fell, as they say. Annette just smiled her weird and sinister metallic smile and Guy suddenly had to tie his shoe, right? Or go to the men's room. There was, as Doctor Plot would write, a strained silence. We all pretended that it was just a normal quarrel, had nothing to do with sex, and so on and so forth. The rest of the night was, well, it was just an ordinary night. Lou and Sheila drove me and Guy home as I remember, we lived near them and just a couple of blocks from each other. I was living in a broken-down tenement, Jesus, the walls were painted this dark blackish-green, I used to think that if you wanted to commit suicide this trap would help you right along. As a matter of fact, Tony Lamont used to call it Felo-de-se Towers.

Did Guy make indecent advances to Sheila in the car?

I suppose you might say that, only I don't know if I'd use the word advances, they were a little more than that, at least from what I could see in the rear-view mirror. Lou was pretty well in the bag and asked me to drive or maybe Sheila did. Anyway, I was driving and Lou was next to me in the front and Sheila and Guy were in the back. O.K. So I could see a little, Lou was just sitting there asleep, maybe. Maybe he was asleep or just pretending. I could see that Guy was kissing Sheila and feeling her up, her breasts and her legs, thighs, you know, I couldn't really see. I suppose he had his hand under her skirt too, I had to keep my eyes on the road, right? I mean I wasn't exactly cold sober either. But I'll tell you that son of a bitch Guy had some moxie because, I mean to say that when I got to his place Lou woke up or as I said maybe he wasn't asleep at all and he pretended to wake up, and Guy tells him that Sheila has the most beautiful legs he's ever seen, I'll tell you there was a hell of a lot of them to see too, and I thought to myself, O.K. Now Lou will *have* to say something, whether he knew what was going on in the back seat or not. Believe me, there was a lot of heavy breathing, they weren't even trying to be discreet, almost as if they, you know, wanted Lou to turn around and catch them, well he didn't. I did. There Lou sat, his eyes closed, while they went at it, if Guy had lived a couple of miles further on they would have made it right there. As for me, hell, they must have known that I could see them but that goddam Sheila, well. No sense in thinking about all that now, what's the old phrase, speak nothing but good of the dead? What was I about to, oh right. When Guy makes this remark about Sheila's legs, and he was right, her legs were, well like that old song goes they'd make a preacher lay his bible down, they started somewhere up around her ribs. He makes this remark and Lou turns around, Jesus Christ almighty! Sheila is straightening her clothes, pulling her skirt down from up around her hips for Christ sake, and Lou says, are they better than Bunny's? I remember that so clearly. Guy is outside the car on the street and he leans in the window for a second, he says, he's got this grim smile on his face, he says, what the fuck would I know about my wife's legs? And the word wife is just, it's just dripping, as they say, with contempt. Then as he starts to turn away by Christ if he doesn't stick his head in the car and look at Sheila. He says, I can't remember exactly, but he says something like thanks for a great evening. Lou is smoking a cigarette and looking into the distance. Happy days. Happy golden days. And it was only the beginning of this thing between Guy and Sheila. As a matter of fact there was another time in Lou's car with Guy and Sheila in the back seat again, they were always in each other's pockets then, this was later, I mean it was after the night I just mentioned, I was in the car in the front with Lou, Lou was doing the driving and I think, yes, Léonie was between us, I was seeing a lot of her then. She was in bad shape with that bastard Tete, that was just about the time he gave her the business by hiring Sylvie Lacruseille, you remember? Luba Checks, to run the boutique. I was trying to persuade Léonie to quit the place and start to write again. I thought that maybe I could get Saul to talk to Lee Jefferson and get her to publish something in *Hip Vox*, nothing came of any of it. Léonie would write a sentence then get up and walk around her apartment and then open the vodka. When I came in she'd start in on me, she would be really abusive. But. But at other times she'd be really beautiful, just, I don't mean to be corny, but just radiant. She was a beautiful woman. This is all so old and vague, so old and dead, I must be crazy even to think about it all. We were seeing each other a lot, I was feeling really low and she was feeling lower if possible, we must have been some pair. I was Mister Joy and she was Miss Laughter. So there we all were in the car, they were on their way to someplace, a party, always a fucking party, we were always en masse in those days. Our Gang. They were driving me and Léonie, if I'm thinking of the right evening, to a lecture, yes, right. A lecture by some member of a radical-lesbian-feminist group, the one I told you about that Ellen was in, the Tribade Conspiracie, spelled with c i e at the end, conspira*cie*, c i e, they thought it was a more feminine ending than a y. What in the name of sweet suffering Jesus we were going for I don't know, we never did get there, but for some reason Léonie thought she should go, it was some sort of talk or panel discussion or colloquium on literary innovation or experimentation or something, the avant-garde being just another repressive tool of the white-male-heterosexual establishment. I imagine you've been here before but it just came back to me. If I wanted I could probably reconstruct the arguments for you cliché by cliché. But anyway. They were going to their party and we were going to this fire-eating discussion that would wind up no doubt by turning Sara Teasdale into the greatest thing since canned beer. O.K. You should know that a little while before this Guy had moved in, sort of moved in with Lou and Sheila, he and Bunny were really on the rocks, they couldn't, as the shining phrase goes, stand the fucking sight of each other. So Guy had, as I say, just *sort* of moved in since he left most of his clothes and things at his place. But he was very much *there* at the Henrys' apartment. He and Sheila must have been jumping into the sack at every opportunity. And Lou ignored it. I guess. Hell, I don't know, maybe he watched for all I know, maybe they had cozy little parties, I wouldn't put much past Sheila. Anyway, in the car I turned around to say something to Guy and they were at it, both, you know, in, their clothes were in disarray, to be discreet. I mean they just didn't, they did *not* give a good goddam, it was really unbelievable. Then Léonie looked around, Sheila was straddling Guy, Lou was just, Jesus Christ! just driving, I think he asked me to find some jazz on the radio, jazz indeed! Léonie asked Lou to stop the car and she got out and pulled me out after her. Lou took off again, staring, you know, straight ahead, and his wife and Guy were just oblivious to everything there in the back seat, just, well, they were just fucking their brains out. I don't know how many times this sort of thing happened in the car, I should say it wasn't just the *car*, it was that the car was a kind of extension of the bedroom. Or the couch or the floor or the closet or the bathroom. Sheila and Guy were just, you know, they were wearing it *out*. And of course the car, well, it was a car accident that killed Sheila but that time, that was one time that Guy wasn't there, he had the flu or something, a virus. That time it was just Lou and Sheila and me.

What were you doing in the car?

Well it was a few months later, let me think. They were on their way to a party, yet another party, and they were dropping me off at the train station. I'd been invited for the weekend, it was a long weekend,

I think it was either Memorial Day or the Fourth of July, it was warm anyway. I'd been invited to Dick and April's beach house for the weekend, Dick was making barrels of money, he had some kind of a business arrangement with Barnett and somebody else, I can't remember who, something to do with limited-run tapestries, or one of a kind wall hangings made from famous paintings or paintings by well-known artists. It was shady, what else would it be with Barnett involved? They didn't bother to get the artists' permissions or the permissions of their estates, they charged some obscene prices for this stuff, most of it went to Latin America, sleazy government officials who didn't know what to do with their loot, I don't know. Anyway, I was going for the weekend. We were driving along when suddenly Sheila starts to take off her clothes and throw them into the front seat, I'm sitting next to Lou and Sheila's dress goes flying, then her slip, her bra, her underpants. Lou stops the car and Sheila for Christ sake gets out! She gets out of the goddam car. She stood right in front of it banging on the hood in nothing but her shoes and stockings, a little garter belt. Lou was crying, it was really grim, then Sheila started to run down the street, people were looking at her, this naked, good as naked woman. Then she ran back toward the car and when she was about twenty feet in front of it, I don't know, it just shot forward and Lou, Lou. The car ran her down. She died. She broke her neck. Jesus Christ. Lou got out and stood there, stood over her, I knew she was dead just the way she got hit, the way she got knocked just flat. Snap. Jesus Christ. We'd been drinking most of the afternoon but Sheila could hold her liquor, I don't know what the hell happened for her to just, to simply freak out the way she did. We were just sitting there, I was sitting right next to her, we were all talking, as a matter of fact we were gossiping about the Detectives, Sheila called them Mister and Mrs. Rolex. Everything seemed very funny, we'd smoked a little grass, you know? Not a hell of a lot of grass. Then all of a sudden Sheila gave me a strange look and reached down to the hem of her dress and pulled it up, her dress, I said hey! Wait a minute! Then she pulled her dress right *off*, she threw it at Lou, then, you know, her underclothes. I tried to stop her from taking her bra off and Lou was, you know, Lou was crazy, he was reaching back to her and driving at the same time. My God. When I tried to hold her arms she butted me in the face with her head, I guess that was when Lou stopped the car and Sheila just jumped out into the street. Lou started to chase her, then he ran back to the car. Then he got back in as I recall. Or it was just before Sheila started to run back toward us that he came back to the car, he asked me to, you know, he gestured, waved his arms, I guess he wanted me to follow them in the car but by the time I reacted, I mean that I had to get into the front seat because I was in the back because I'd got back there when Sheila threw her dress at Lou, at the both of us, to try and stop her from going really, well, really crazy, right? By the time I got into the front seat again Lou was back in the car and Sheila was standing there about twenty feet away in the headlights, laughing and screaming and cursing like a madwoman and giving me the finger, or the both of us, I don't know. Then the car just, Jesus Christ. I remember, so clearly, sitting there in the front listening to "Scrapple from the Apple," it's odd what you remember.

What was the occasion for the party to which they were going?

Jesus, I don't know. It wasn't actually a party, it was a reception at a bookstore for Cecil Tyrell to honor the publication of his *Orange Steel*. Sheila didn't even want to go. She hated Cecil, I told you that, I think.

There have been persistent rumors that Lou Henry owed something to Guy Lewis and that this debt was the reason that Guy was tolerated as a more or less permanent guest in Lou's home. What, if anything, did Lou owe Guy?

As far as I know, he owed him nothing. Lou was a mark and Guy was a manipulator. Besides, Guy wasn't a permanent, as you say, guest, and it was Sheila who invited him, really. They were hot for each other, O.K.? As simple as that. Sheila was a, let's say she was a free spirit.

What was Sheila wearing?

What was she wearing. Let me, I don't think I really remember, but it might have been a pale-blue dress, or maybe lavender. She had a dress like that that she wore to, you know, special, if you will, special parties. Very soft filmy material, maybe it was silk, I think that was it, that particular pale-blue dress, but it's hard to remember. All I see when I think of it is Sheila in those damn headlights in nothing but her shoes and stockings, her clothes, I don't, and her other clothes, I mean her underclothes, it seems to me that they, her slip and other things were white. They were, yes, probably white. Sheila always wore white underwear, very plain, chaste. What a word. But I think that was it. She had on white underclothes and that very soft, that very soft pale-blue dress. I don't remember her shoes. Heels, but I don't remember them.

Earlier you mentioned, in passing, that there had been a lot of drinking. What sort of drinking?

Just, hell, you know, drinking. It was, it had to be a Friday afternoon, early afternoon, I went over to Lou and Sheila's with my bag, because as I said, they were going to give me a lift to the station. I was a little surprised because when I got there Pungoe and Annie Flammard were there in the living room and it was, well, you know that feeling you get when people have been talking about something they don't want you to know about. That was how it was, I came in and everybody just shut up. They all seemed well on the way so I poured myself a big drink, gin on the rocks I think, a new taste thrill. Hell, I don't know, we started talking about all sorts of things, it was strictly social. So it seemed to me. Then we I guess smoked a little grass, actually it was hash, Annie had a big piece of it, she was, I think, dealing at the time. Maybe not. It doesn't matter. We all got stoned anyway. I imagine that I was hoping to get so wasted that I'd miss the train because the last thing on earth I wanted to do was spend a weekend with Dick and April, you know? They'd told me they had a great time planned and when the Detectives planned things, run do not walk to the nearest exit. It was strictly murder in the henhouse. They gave a, they called it a winter carnival once at their place in Vermont, dear sweet Christ! That was a kind of parody of a comedy of manners if you can imagine such a thing. A lot of sex and jealousy and weeping, people sick and depressed. Well, that's got nothing to do with all this. The point is that we were all feeling, as they say, no pain. Pungoe and Annie for some reason seemed especially smug, I don't quite know how to say it, the cat that ate the canary. So we were smoking and drinking, listening to some music, and I recall that we were talking about Henri's novel, *Mouth of Steel*, because Lou had, I think, just got a catalogue from a book dealer, modern first editions, you know, and Henri's book was listed, a presentation copy Lou said, at five hundred dollars. I've often wondered who sold Henri's book. Anyway, this and that, we just talked. After a couple of hours Pungoe and Annie said they had to go and then Sheila went into the bedroom to get dressed. I sat with Lou and Christ knows, I think Lou started to complain and bitch and moan about, what else? Guy. I didn't want to hear this. Besides, I figured Guy would come out from under the couch for Christ sake, the man who came to dinner. Guy wasn't there though, as I said, he was sick or something. Where he was I don't know and I didn't give a good goddam. I can't begin to tell you how disgusted I was with all the, with everything, with everybody, it was all just, I don't know how to describe it. Just shit, you know? Shit. I really hated every motherfucking one of them, men and women and myself included. I went into the bathroom because I could see that Lou was getting ready to cry all over me about his whore of a wife and how much he adored her and I didn't need it. I'm in the bathroom washing my hands and face, wasting time, stoned but not that stoned and I see an envelope on the floor, a manila envelope propped between the toilet and the back wall, so I pick it up. I'm not really a snooper but something, oh hell, I don't know, who the hell cares anyway, I open the thing. O.K. Inside there's a bunch of color photographs. One shows a table around which there are four men, the great Pungoe, Barnett and Horace, and a fourth guy I didn't recognize, but he really didn't look like a man, more like a woman dressed like a man, short black hair, no make-up. Anyway. There's a lamp in the corner. It was obvious, I should add, that it was taken in Horace's apartment. O.K. There's a lamp in the corner and under the lamp a pile of clothes, they looked like women's clothes but I really couldn't tell. Then there's a second photograph, the same four looking at a woman with her back to the camera, she's naked except for a pair of black high-heeled boots and a black slouch hat, a wide-brimmed hat and the third picture, the woman is on her hands and knees and the guy who doesn't look like a guy at all is giving it to her from behind, he's still completely dressed. The other three, dear pals all, Harlan, Horace and Barnett are still at the table watching. You couldn't tell who the woman was at all because of her big hat. So I'm looking at these photos, thinking that they must have something to do with Annie, but what the hell are they doing here? One thing I *could* tell was that the woman wasn't Sheila, I mean because Sheila, Sheila wouldn't do such a thing, you can say that for her despite her, well, her appetites. Then there were five more photographs, taken outdoors, Christ knows where, trees and shrubs, flowers, a formal English garden, it could have been anywhere. The pictures were of, let me think, Vance, Jack Towne, Jesus yes, Jack, and he looked wonderful, Lincoln Gom, John Hicks, that creepy bastard, and who else? I can't remember the fifth one but it was a man, they were all men. Who the hell? I really can't remember. There was also, of all things, a dust-jacket picture, I mean clipped from a dust-jacket, of the woman I told you about, the critical work? Ann T. Redding. Doctor Redding. Same picture I'd seen in the library, so somebody else must have been curious about the name and that rumor about Annette. Something like that or else why would they have the picture? I put everything back where it had been and went out to the living room. I was thinking of mentioning it to Lou, not that I'd looked at the stuff, I felt a little sleazy about that, but just that there was an envelope in the bathroom, you know, as if maybe he'd dropped it or Pungoe or Annie had dropped it, but Sheila was ready and I just let it go. We had a few more drinks and Sheila made some sandwiches and we had a bite then we, as I said, we left. I wish I could remember that fifth man but I'll be damned if I can.

The seating arrangement in the car?

I thought I told you? Well, maybe not really. It was a little confused, complicated I suppose. When we got to the car Sheila told me to sit in the back by myself, she was very very chilly toward me. I should say cold, ice cold. I don't know why but she turned it right on. Asking me, excuse me, *telling* me to sit in the back was but one manifestation, as they say, of her displeasure. O.K. For some reason, maybe because he was drunk, Lou decided to be masterful, Mister Husband. So after a couple of blocks he pulled over and said he wanted to talk to me and he'd be goddamned if he was going to keep turning around all the time. Sheila didn't say a word, she got out, I got out. Then she got in the back and I got in the front. But, oh Christ! the whole thing was absolutely ridiculous. The crazy woman refused to close the door until I got *back* into the back with her. I could see Lou was about to break his jaws grinding his teeth, right? I was going to just say fuck the both of you and get a cab when Lou says, all right, humor her, the bitch, something like that. All right. She and I are in the back and she starts to get amorous. To be blunt, she starts to grope me, feel me up, but she's being obvious the way she acted with Guy. You know, she's acting as if it's all a big joke so that Lou can see that there's nothing, what shall I say? nothing furtive. Fun on the road! Anyway. Anyway. Christ, this is all so futile. Anyway, I objected to this, you know, all this hearty laughter while the smoke is coming out of my ears and I'm about to bust through my pants like the guys in the dirty comic books. Oh God, Sheila. So I finally got back in the front seat and the next thing was, I told you the next thing. Sheila started to undress.

Was it still twilight, or had it already grown dark?

When we started out it was still a little light, that very pale light, but when Sheila got hit, when she got hit we, she was in the headlights. So it was almost dark, but not quite. It was also sort of misty, a kind of very quiet, very beautiful night. It rained later. But at that time, earlier, it was absolutely lovely, still, and in a way very mysterious, peaceful. The really curious thing about it was that after Sheila was dead, they came, they took her to the hospital and pronounced her dead, this curious thing came into my mind. It had to do with Leo's novel, *Isolate Flecks*, you know, Leo Kaufman. There's a scene in the book that describes a foggy, misty night in the city just like that night. And Sheila used to laugh her head off over that passage. She'd say that it was a perfect example of Leo's way out of all problems, she'd say, look at that stupid book! When Leo gets stuck he always describes nature. I'm damned if she wasn't right and the fog business, the mist, all that garbage for some reason that especially amused her. Really tickled her. Anyway, what I was getting at is that it occurred to me later that night sitting with Lou in the dark, drinking, I mean it occurred to me, I wondered if Sheila remembered that scene when she was out in the street. I wonder if she did.

What was left in the dresser in The Red Swan Inn?

In the top left drawer: a small toy tin pig wearing a sailor suit and carrying a drum; a postcard depicting a view of San Francisco taken from Twin Peaks on the back of which is written in blue ink the word "cupcakes"; a pink paper napkin on which is crudely printed the image of a filled cocktail glass from which bubbles rise and the words HELEN AND TROY'S OHIO'S FREINDLIEST COCKTAIL LOUNGE; a peach-colored silk slip with white lace hem and bodice.

In the second left drawer: a slender pamphlet entitled "Sexology: 100 Facts"; a book of matches on which is printed LENTO'S BAR AND GRILLE STEAKS CHOPS PIZZA SANDWICHES FINE LIQUORS; an empty Bromo-Seltzer bottle; a peach-colored silk slip with white lace hem and bodice.

In the third left drawer: a color slide of an abstract expressionist painting entitled *The Valley of the Shadow of Death*; a photograph of three young girls on a parched lawn, one wearing a summer dress and the others pullovers and short pants; an issue of a film magazine called *Flikk*; a peach-colored silk slip with white lace hem and bodice.

In the bottom left drawer: a brittle sepia-tone photograph of four women and two men, dressed in white, playing lawn croquet; a garishly colored post card depicting a large hotel with two of its windows each marked with an "X" in black ink, on the back of which is written, in the same black ink, "We're having *some* fun!! See you soon. Love, The Kids"; a photograph of a black man sitting on a bed cradling a tenor saxophone in his arms; a peach-colored silk slip with white lace hem and bodice.

In the top right drawer: a scorecard of a baseball game between two semipro teams, the Crystals and the Ambers, noting that the game was called after three full innings of play for unknown reasons; a throwaway brochure claiming that Mrs. Louise Ashby, a Healer,

Reader, Adviser, Seeress, and Prophet, will reveal the sickness that is in you; a children's book entitled *The Daddy and the Drake* by Louis Condy with watercolors by "Georgette"; a peach-colored silk slip with white lace hem and bodice.

In the second right drawer: a photograph of a ten-year-old boy with a crossed left eye holding a kitten up as if for our inspection; an unopened package of Camel cigarettes; a leather tobacco pouch half-filled with tobacco; a peach-colored silk slip with white lace hem and bodice.

In the third right drawer: three decks of Tarot cards: the Tarot of Marseilles; the Tarot of Oswald Wirth; the Tarot of Arthur Edward Waite illustrated by Pamela Colman Smith; a peach-colored silk slip with white lace hem and bodice.

In the bottom right drawer: a short French novel entitled *La Musique et les mauvaises herbes*; a newspaper clipping of an interview with a congressman's wife; a black-and-white drawing of an extraordinarily odd-looking wagon or cart; a black silk slip with black lace hem and bodice.

Can you give me any more information on her?

Soon after being granted her Ph.D. from the University of Chicago—her dissertation was titled "Sexual Desire as Evidenced in Selected Phonemic Groupings in Virginia Woolf's *Mrs. Dalloway*"—Dr. Redding was discovered in a compromising situation with First Lieutenant Evelyn Leonard of the Women's Army Corps at the New Ecstasy Motor Inn outside Webster Groves, Missouri.

Dr. Redding later denied that it had been she and strongly implied that the woman in bed with Lieutenant Leonard had been her twin sister, Phyllis Redding, the manager of the Naughty Nightie boutique in nearby Kirkwood and a locally well-known champion of unpopular liberal causes.

Eight years later, Dr. Redding became the President of the radical-feminist organization, The Daughters of Durga International, and two years after that was awarded an honorary membership in the radical-lesbian organization, the Tribade Conspiracie.

To what thing or place or idea or whatever does the title, *99*, that she gave to that sculpture, refer?

Annie Flammard made six sculptures: *Blackjack, Amber Glass, Lorzu, The Caliph, Ten Eyck Walk*, and *The Metallic Fly*.

What was the name of the fifth person in the series of erotic photographs found in the bathroom by him?

Pamela Ann Johanssen, an aspiring actress, whose professional name was Pamela Clairwil.

She had been one of the earliest members of the Tribade Conspiracie, but had been expelled from that organization for "pandering to base male fantasies of the lesbian way of life."

Then if it wasn't Ward, what *was* her maiden name?

Harlan.

Joanne Jeanne Judith "Bunny" Harlan.

Was he Ellen Marowitz's father, or was he her brother?

Jack Marowitz, born Jacob Marowitz, was the real name of Jackie Moline, the owner of a small bar-café called The Black Basement, which was, in actuality, a drop for stolen goods.

He had two sisters, Sheila, who married Louis Henry, and Sandra, her identical twin, who was, for twelve years, an assistant to the creative director of a Tel Aviv advertising agency.

She disappeared while scouting locations outside a small village near the Lebanese border.

Jack Marowitz had no children.

Can you give me a description of her so-called "metal" apartment?

Annette Lorpailleur had no apartment of her own, "metal" or otherwise.

She lived in a suite that consisted of a sitting room, a bedroom, and a bathroom in the large cooperative apartment owned by Harlan Pungoe, whose maid, mistress, and confidante she was for six and a half years.

After leaving Mr. Pungoe's employ, she depended on the kindness and good will of friends for her living accommodations.

Then what *is* the novel about?

Blackjack deals with a scandal centered on a respected teacher of creative writing at a major university who steals characters, ideas, plots, themes, and even locales from his students and uses those materials useful to him to write his own stories, which he publishes in literary magazines of limited circulation under a pseudonym, John Black.

Ultimately, he publishes a collection of these stories to extremely favorable reviews, sells the book to a paperback publisher and a film producer, and is honored by the award of three prestigious literary prizes to the collection.

At this point, the teacher's true identity becomes known, and his ex-students sue him for plagiary.

He retains a brilliant and beautiful woman lawyer who successfully defends him by demonstrating, in court, that the stories that the teacher has purportedly plagiarized, as well as the stories written and published by him, are almost identical, in theme, construction, and technique, with thirty-three stories, selected from five nationally known magazines, published over the five-year period preceding the trial.

Her defense of her client lucidly and penetratingly argues that any one work of popular fiction is substantially the same as all other works of popular fiction.

The teacher is acquitted and the novel ends with him and the lawyer registering at a charming country inn as "Mr. and Mrs. Jack Black."

Was the book written by Annette Lorpailleur or by Henri Kink?

La Bouche métallique or *Mouth of Steel* was written by Annette Lorpailleur.

The only known work by Henri Kink is a poem that appeared in a long-defunct little magazine, *Blue Filter*.

It is titled "Poem" and reads:

What are the various fragments of memory?
—bits of dark sky or silk in a drawer
and dead voices from old photos
on the walls: bitter inventory.

I am a man with a notebook who
thinks himself sane, I am probably sane
but assaulted by these shards of the bizarre,
these phenomena of decay.

So that my voice is trapped
with the lost voices in the photographs
suddenly my body fades smudged
into the pieces of sky faded blacker—

Are the accounts that I've been given of their deaths and disappearances substantially correct?

No.

None of these people has either died or disappeared.

Vance Whitestone and Lincoln Gom jointly own a small, lucrative costume shop, The Good Company, that supplies costumes for sale or rent.

Their most popular items are: Saucy French Maid, Naughty Nurse, Blushing Nun, Cute Cop, Boss Lady, and Madame Doctor.

Jackson Towne is the day bartender at a chic and expensive cocktail lounge, Caliph's Walk.

Sheila Henry has just published her first book of poems, *Fretwork*.

John Hicks is an advocate for homosexual rights whose weekly column appears in the magazine, *Toujours Gai*.

Henri Kink is an assistant producer for the daytime television serial, *A Waste of Shame*.

What were the particulars of the scandal attendant upon his marriage to Sylvie Lacruseille?

There was no scandal.

There was no marriage.

Such a marriage would have been, and is manifestly impossible.

Dr. John Rube is a fictional character.

Sylvie Lacruseille, *née* Luba Checks, is a real human being.

And what were her duties, if you'll pardon the word, when she worked for Blanche Neige Press?

Marcella Butler never worked for Blanche Neige Press.

The women who worked there were: Lorna Flambeaux, Tania Crosse, and Lena Schmidt.

April Detective occasionally worked for the press on a freelance basis.

You mean that the so-called factual data used by one of my informants were tampered with before my investigation began?

Yes, but not enough of the data to change substantially the information that was given you.

Much of the tampering, if you will, had to do with the chronology of and participants in certain events, changed by persons unknown for reasons that are not at this time wholly clear.

May I see the floor plan of Horace Rosette's apartment?

Then they were *not* the producers of *The Party*?

No.

The Party was produced by a partnership incorporated as White Sun Talent Associates, Inc.

The partnership consisted of three men, Janos Kooba, an emigré from Yugoslavia; Edward Beshary, an ex-professor of linguistics who had left his university post under the cloud of a vaguely defined charge of moral turpitude; and Albert Pearson, an unemployed society-band drummer.

These three had made a fortune in the development of a complex board game, based on the Tarot, the Ouija board, and basic elements of goetic practice, and marketed as The Fool's Paradise.

The film, *The Party*, was vastly and almost unrecognizably different from its original script, written by Craig Garf, and starred Florence Claire, Tamara Flynn, Chet Kendrick, and Thompson Richie.

It opened to savagely bad reviews but currently enjoys a certain cult status among those who claim to see in it a subtle existential dread and an unintentionally strange innocence.

Can you describe this old photograph?

It is a photograph of Dr. Ann Taylor Redding taken when she was eleven years old.

She is sitting cross-legged in the middle of a formal English garden behind a large frame house and she wears a short-sleeved light-colored summer dress, anklets, and Mary Jane shoes.

In her right hand there is an ice-cream cone, partially consumed.

She smiles into the camera.

Across the street, parked by the yard of a neighbor's house, is an old Chevrolet coupe, and in the yard three girls, about the same age as Dr. Redding, are sitting side by side.

Two of them are wearing dresses and one a pullover and short pants.

They are smiling at a club-footed man who is standing about ten feet in front of them, gesturing with one hand.

In his other hand he holds a camera.

What does the phrase "metallic constructions" mean?

Metallic Constructions is an inaccurate, or perhaps more fairly, an unsatisfactory translation of a technical work on engineering, *Les Constructions métalliques*, by Gaspard Monge, the inventor of descriptive geometry.

Monsieur Monge was also the author of a famous—or infamous—novel of the Décadence, *Une Nouvelle Dimension*, published in 1874.

This work is usually attributed to Philothée O'Neddy, since Monge published it under the pseudonym of Théophile Dondey, which was O'Neddy's real name.

Appalled by this cavalier appropriation of his identity, O'Neddy, or Dondey, challenged Monge to a duel in which the latter was killed.

Can you tell me why I was directed to ask my fifth informant the same questions, in reverse order, that I asked my third informant?

No.

What sort of things were strewn about on the study floor?

A sleeveless shift of off-white raw silk, a black evening gown of some shiny metallic fabric, a gray tweed skirt and jacket, a black-and-white-figured rayon scarf, a pale blue silk tailored blouse, smoke-shade nylon stockings, beige nylon stockings, black silk full-fashioned stockings, white nylon panties with white lace trim, a black lace corselette, white cotton panties, a pink silk sleeveless dress, a white lace French garter belt, a white nylon garter belt with lace front panel, a white nylon brassiere, a white cotton brassiere, black sling high-heeled shoes, black stiletto-heeled pumps of some shiny metal, tan stack-heeled shoes with small silver buckles, a tortoiseshell barrette, a pair of glasses with tortoiseshell frames, an orange silk dress, and a habit and wimple of the kind worn by the Sisters of Charity.

Was she a real nun?

Rose Zeppole was a registered nurse who worked for twelve

years in the small clinic of a year-round vacation resort, Blue Runes, which catered to honeymooners and singles.

She is presently nurse and companion to Lena Schmidt, a victim of traumatic or psychosomatic blindness.

Miss Schmidt is the director of a prestigious art gallery that specializes in contemporary metal sculptures, or, more precisely, constructions.

Then there *was* a body found there?

Yes.

The police identified the body as that of Karen Ostrom, an executive secretary who had recently resigned from her job at White Sun Talent Associates, Inc.

Miss Ostrom had falsely registered at The Red Swan as Jeannette Grande, but the police have yet to find a motive for her doing so, or indeed to find a motive for her registering at all.

Her luggage consisted only of an attaché case that contained, according to the police, "a diary, an appointment book, an address book, and a heavily corrected typescript of what seems to be a confidential business report in a pale blue file folder."

Do you think it odd or suspicious that so many of the people who have turned up in our investigation have French—or what seem to be French—names?

No.

It is not our investigation.

Was she a novelist or a boutique manager—or was her name but a pseudonym used by a writer, by some—by *any* writer?

Sylvie Lacruseille worked as a registered nurse for fourteen years, after which she became a very expensive prostitute who serviced clients, both male and female, who had what might be called exotic sexual tastes.

She is currently married to Barnett Tete and is extremely popular and active as the chairwoman of several cultural and charitable organizations, as well as being the founder and president of an inner-city housing-renovation group, Concrete Proposals.

What do you mean by "personal treasures and keepsakes and such"?

For instance, behind the bar of the Red Silk restaurant, the owner has a perfect scale-model of the interior of the Red Silk restaurant, made by Bart Kahane out of toothpicks.

Horace Rosette has a key-ring charm of gold and cloisonné that represents one of his most famous anthologies, *Bridges: Poets Express Their Love.*

Harlan Pungoe carries a tiny pair of black bikini panties with black lace trim in the change purse of his wallet.

Tania Crosse has, on her bedroom dresser, a beautiful doll dressed as Sister Rose Zeppole in her role in *Sisters in Shame.*

Dr. Ann Taylor Redding has, on her desk, a small brass figurine of the Hindu goddess, Durga.

Antony Lamont has a sepia print, greatly reduced, of a rare photograph of James Joyce reclining on a couch dressed in his wife, Nora's, clothes.

Guy and Bunny Lewis have in their bathroom a novelty ash tray, in the shape of a toilet bowl, that plays the Victor Herbert song, "Beautiful Dreamer," when the seat is lifted.

Barnett Tete has a virtually priceless drawing by Fragonard showing the poet Horace writing in a mirror-lined room and surrounded by harlots in wantonly abandoned poses.

Lolita Kahane has a small wooden crucifix, blessed by Pope Pius XII, on the back of which is printed, in faded blue ink, FLINT, CITY OF PROMISE.

Sheila Henry has a pornographic love letter of four typed, single-spaced pages sent her by an anonymous female admirer.

Roger Whytte-Blorenge has a pair of Annette Lorpailleur's black ankle-strap high-heeled shoes.

April and Dick Detective have a first edition presentation copy of *Roberte ce soir*, on the flyleaf of which is written, "À mon prochain Donatien, Toujours, Pierre 1953."

Chico Zeek has, on the wall above his bed, a photograph of

Barry Gatto in his role as Duke Washington in *Hellions in Hosiery*, inscribed, "To 'Chico' with love, Baylor."

Marcella Butler has the heavily corrected typescript of a poem by Roberte Flambeaux titled "Renée-Pélagie: The Ecstasy of Her Agony."

Duke Washington has the alto-saxophone reed used by Sonny Stitt on the famous original recording of "Ko-Ko."

Dick Detective has at least one photograph of everyone he has ever known.

Barnett Tete has the original manuscript, stolen from the Bibliothèque Nationale, and substituted for by a perfect forgery, of Monge's *Géométrie descriptive.*

Guy Lewis has a photograph, taken by a Baby Brownie, of Ann Taylor Redding, at the age of eleven, standing in the rose garden of her family's home in Webster Groves, Missouri.

Lee Jefferson has a complete set of repro proofs of the first number of *Lorzu*, inscribed: "To Zooz from her adoring slave, Craig."

Lincoln Gom has the prints and negatives of a series of erotic photographs of Tania Crosse with an unidentified man and woman taken the week before she became the manager of the Soirée Intime.

Lena Schmidt has a copperplated ear trumpet that once belonged to her grandmother, Helga Schmidt McGrath.

Anne Kaufman has the manuscript of a piece of juvenilia by Leo Kaufman, a short story called "Sleeping With the Lions."

Lucy Taylor has a pink latex dildo that she calls "Big Yank."

Page Moses has an empty manila file folder labeled THE PARTY, given him by a private investigator, Donald Plot.

Guy Lewis has a set of keys to a car once owned by Lou Henry.

Léonie Aubois has three curiously affectionate fan letters, given to her as a present by Barnett Tete, from Herbert Hoover to Tom Mix.

Annette Lorpailleur has a gold medallion into which is meticulously incised the seal of the demon Paimon.

Cecil Tyrell has four scrapbooks filled with more than five hundred articles clipped from newspapers and magazines over a twenty-year period, all of which bear the title, "The Avant-Garde: Finally Dead?"

Barry Gatto has a full-dress uniform of an officer of the Peruvian Army, complete with braids, medals, and sash.

Sheila Henry has her own Certificate of Death in a frame on her dresser.

Conchita Kahane has her high school Spanish primer, *Primer Curso de Español*.

Biggs Richard has an untitled and unsigned manuscript of eight hundred and twelve pages, found in a taxi, that purports to prove conclusively that all artists, throughout recorded history, were actively or latently homosexual.

Karen Ostrom has a toy airplane on whose wings is printed the legend, WELCOME TO KANSAS CITY.

There are many more which it is pointless to catalogue.

What is the importance of this catalogue to my investigation?

If the catalogue, or any catalogue or list, is understood to be a system, its entropy is the measure of the unavailability of its energy for conversion into useful work.

The ideal catalogue tends toward maximum entropy.

Stick it in your ear.

What titles might best describe the study I will undoubtedly write on these people and their relationships?

White Shifts, Permanent Guests, Envelopes, Consensus, Acquisitions, Heavy Machinery, Labors of Love, Doubles Cross, Odd Numerals, Indelible Experiences, Strange Coincidences, Complicated Webs, Qualifications, Lack of Evidence, A Grain of Salt, Blinding Clarity, Construction in Metal, Twilights, Dead Beats, Environments, Parts of the Gangs, Cults and Coteries, Reams and Reams, Complex Resolutions, Little Cabals, Ventriloquists' Dummies, Official Mouths, Set Pieces, Farfetched, Cameras Work, Accidental Bodies, Lens and Shutter, Growing Dark.

Why is there such a dearth of information on her?

Because of the ignominious manner in which she was permanently crippled.

While drunkenly slopping hogs for her husband, Antonia Harley fell into the sty and was attacked and badly injured by two boars, Homer and Dante, and a sow, Sappho.

Why was it his favorite book?

Harlan Pungoe believes that *A Pack of Lies*, which he knew almost by heart, and quoted from daily, helped him to keep his essentially American values intact despite the unavoidable and occasionally unfortunate business dealings that involved him in fraud, forgery, blackmail, arson, extortion, drugs, rape, prostitution, assault, murder, and what he somewhat obscurely referred to as Christian pornography.

How long did he spend in the mental hospital before being released as an outpatient?

Bart Kahane was never in a mental hospital, either as an inpatient or an outpatient.

He has been in a hospital for the past thirteen years in a deep coma subsequent to a jump from a third-floor window of a cheap hotel, the Lincoln Inn, during the course of a fire that totally destroyed the structure.

The jump was the cause of a ruptured spleen, a broken leg, two broken arms, six broken ribs, and massive brain injuries.

What *about* the quality of the information given me by my other informants?

It is somewhat distorted by omissions, exaggerations, inventions, fantasies, confusions, prejudices, egoism, faulty memories, contradictions, and outright lies.

May I *please* see the floor plan of Harlan Pungoe's apartment?

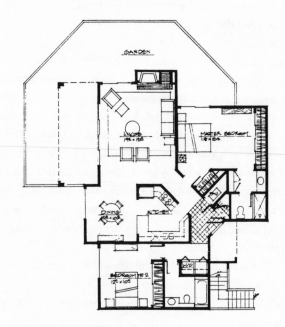

What were the names of the demons invoked?

BAAL, who imparts invisibility and cunning.

SEERE, who brings things to pass suddenly, transports to any place in a split second, and distorts messages.

HAGENTI, who grants wisdom, transmutes all metals into gold, and turns water into wine.

OSE, who gives skill in all abstruse sciences and true answers concerning secret things, who can change human beings into any shape that the magician may desire, so that those that are changed will not know it, and who can also reduce them to such a state of insanity that they will believe their identity changed, which delusion will last for as long as the magician may desire.

PHOENIX, who speaks marvelously of all arts, proves an excellent poet, and fulfills all and any orders admirably.

PAIMON, who speaks with a distant voice, teaches the arts of metamorphosis, gives and confirms wealth and dignities, and makes human beings subject to the will of the magician.

SYTRY, who procures sexual love of all kinds, and causes women to show themselves naked, *jussus secreta libenter detegit feminarum, eas ridens ludificansque ut se luxorise nudent.*

What do you mean by "perhaps more important papers" on his desk?

On his desk there is a manuscript, a typescript, to be precise, of a little more than a hundred and fifty pages.

It is heavily corrected in pencil, blue ink, and black ink, with numerous interlinear and marginal addenda, and rests in a pale blue file folder which is neither marked nor labeled.

Next to the manuscript is a single sheet of white paper on which there is typed a paragraph that reads:

On his desk there is a manuscript, a typescript, to be precise, of a little more than a hundred and fifty pages.

It is heavily corrected in pencil, blue ink, and black ink, with numerous interlinear and marginal addenda, and rests in a pale blue file folder which is neither marked nor labeled.

Next to the manuscript is a single sheet of white paper on which there is typed a paragraph that reads:

Design by David Bullen
Typeset in Mergenthaler Walbaum
by Wilsted & Taylor
Printed by Maple-Vail
on acid-free paper